Cold Case Chaos

Historical Fiction

Based on a True Story

by

Conrad Case

and

M. Peggy A. Rew

Splash Books

Reno, NV

LRPNV.COM

"If you are locking for a book that takes you on twists, turns with mystery and fantastical wordsmithing...Cold Case Chaos is for you! I loved this book! And you will, too...trust me and the talented detective team."

~Dr. Terry Chase, ND, MA, RN, CEIP-ED,
Speaker, Author & Coach

"An alluring story about uncovering the truth-- not just who the killer was, but why they thought justice had to come at the cost of blood."

~Tammie Jo Cox, Mystery Lover &
Northern Nevada Real Estate agent

Dedication:

To Peggy:

Thanks to her expertise for getting this project going and completed.

~Conrad

To Conrad:

And suddenly you just knew it was time to trust the magic of new beginnings and be thrilled with the endgame.

~Peggy

Acknowledgment:

I also want to thank **Conrad** for the opportunity to ghostwrite, then co-author an awesome story. Deep-diving into Glassport, PA. gave me incredible, historical insight into events of this borough and nearby towns, its people, transit, local businesses, the magnificent rivers and maps. Akin to Northern Nevada, the weather will always be part of Glassport's quintessential charm and usually a bossy player in every day's activity. I now long to visit.

Veracious editing confidants are invaluable for butt-kicking any author to the finish line, so many thanks to my scarlet quill cohorts: husband-counterpoint, **Dale Rew** and bodice-ripping, erotic romance sculptor-pal, **Lynda Bailey**.

~Peggy

1 ~

Gritty Groundwork

Mother Nature had been cranky lately, and a peculiar, almost celestial fog had rolled into town the night before, cloaking dusky streets and shrouding timeworn secrets long buried with morning mist as it conveyed dubious whispers of the past, promising to rendezvous with the present daybreak.

No matter which direction it took, Glassport's Lieutenant Detective Kelly O'Malley loved to walk to work anyway. He enjoyed being a part of the Main Street morning multitude.

He strolled down the sidewalk of the four-lane avenue, his gaze lingering on the fresh asphalt pavement laid just last week, noting how it sparkled and shimmered with an almost ethereal quality in the lingering misty haze. Recent street renovations had all but erased some of the rich history of the southwestern borough, yet everywhere you looked in town, improvements were still undeniably needed. Gone, too, were the mismatched steel-gray and reddish-brown brick streets, replaced by this smooth, dark surface. The artery pulsed a sense of order, courtesy of its white margins. The old streetcar tracks that had once served as vital transportation, running north and south like iron veins through the town, were now just relics of a time long past.

Before the age of electricity, Glassport had honored horse-drawn streetcars, a charming mode of transport providing residents with access to nearly anywhere in town yet always maintained a direct route to the bustling metropolis of Pittsburgh, a mere ten miles to the north. Now, buses, their tires splashing through the morning puddles, were the primary conveyance for the steady stream of commuters heading to the big city.

As he continued down Monongahela Avenue, the doors of many small businesses began creaking open, welcoming the start of a soggy, yet undeniably beautiful day. Although the faint, sharp tang of dry-cleaning chemicals momentarily drifted in the air, the subsequent fresh, clean scent served as a mental note for him to collect his suits soon. The owner of the local copy shop offered him a cheerful wave through the glass, and then, the unexpected and potent aroma of the Donut Doozy was an undeniable assault on his defenseless olfactory senses.

Try as he might, O'Malley couldn't ignore the hypnotic lure of the Doozy's offerings: the warm, sweet scent of cinnamon and vanilla, the nutty fragrance of toasted almonds, and the rich aroma of freshly brewed coffee all mingled in the air.

He stepped inside, a wry smile playing on his lips. "You gals got me again! Does my wife somehow tell you which days I choose to walk to work?"

"No, sir, but we've learned your passive resistance always crumbles in the face of our baked goodies," Daisy replied, her voice cheerful as she sported a silly donut bonnet adorned with colorful sprinkles.

"Fine, you win. I'll take a chocolate iced bar for myself, and a cherry turnover to-go for the captain."

Back out on the sidewalk, the morning pace had quickened; more people were now scurrying every which way, causing the quiet little town to buzz with a bit more workday energy.

As O'Malley arrived at police headquarters, he glanced at the old beige brick building. Its architecture was more reminiscent of a 1950s apartment house than a thrumming center of law enforcement activity. The structure clearly needed updating, but the county taxes were kept low, deliberately, for the locals, especially considering the steady decline in the town's population over the past decades.

Heading directly upstairs to Captain Lance Grey's office, he hung his well-worn Bilby hat and drizzled overcoat on the creaky wooden rack. "Captain, good morning. I brought you a local offering. I also gathered from our efficient switchboard you were looking for me today."

"O'Malley, good morning to you too. And wow, a cherry turnover. Precisely what my waistline didn't need, but I certainly won't refuse." Captain Grey chuckled, accepting the pastry. "I see your current caseload has finally lightened up, which is opportune because I have a special assignment for you. Mayor Hogan wants us to form a dedicated cold case unit, and Chief Mooney personally selected you for the task, citing your excellent case-solving record. Those were his exact words. We know retirement has been on your mind, so solve this case, and there will be a significant bonus in it for you. Perhaps enough to finally purchase a beach cabana somewhere warm. This town still holds so many hidden mysteries, and it's high time we started to unravel them. And we'll begin with this one." He slid a manila folder across his cluttered desk.

"A cold case unit, Captain? Seriously? I'm somewhat surprised our little town even warrants a cold case unit. Why the sudden interest now?" O'Malley asked, a hint of skepticism in his voice.

"This singular case is a bit unusual, so sit down so we can discuss the details while we devour these delightful treats." Captain Grey gestured to the chairs opposite his desk.

"The mayor's older brother, Arthur Hogan, served in the Korean War alongside a man named Karl Schmidt. Schmidt, by all accounts, was a local ruffian whose character only seemed to deteriorate with age. He was killed here in town on the night of October 17th, 1970. For some rather odd reason, the mayor's family started reminiscing about it during a recent family dinner, and now they've decided they want to know who did it, even though no one in town really cared or talked about it. Our only lead from twenty-five years ago was a young woman named Jody Larmi, who had made threats against Schmidt back then. The original investigative team interrogated her, and she thoroughly explained the circumstances surrounding a rather unpleasant neighborhood BBQ incident back in 1962. She even passed a polygraph test."

Captain Grey finished his turnover with a satisfied sigh. "The investigative team at the time believed her account, had no other viable suspects, and consequently, the case went cold. Here's the case file." He tapped the manila folder. "Familiarize yourself with these notes, and hopefully, your fresh perspective can uncover a few unreported specifics. Anything at all, O'Malley. Even the smallest detail could be significant."

"Wow, this will certainly be a challenge." O'Malley picked up the file. "After I review these old documents, I'll try to track down this Jody Larmi."

2 ~

Glassport Gossip

Nestled amongst the verdant, rolling hills of southwestern Pennsylvania, Glassport might initially appear to vacationers or those simply passing through as a quaint and peaceful town.

However, beneath its serene facade lies a history rich with eccentricities and whispered secrets, as jagged and fragmented as the pieces of colored glass thrusted and wedged into the curved banks of the Monongahela River. These unexpected treasures, catching the sunlight with a muted sparkle, are the remnants of a bygone era, birthed from the fiery furnaces of the old glass company that once defined this town.

Lush, continuous forests, a tapestry of emerald, deep moss and patina, hold a hypnotic allure for backpackers, families enjoying leisurely trail walks, and daily local ramblers like O'Malley. The intricate entanglement of hiking paths, shaded by a canopy of native trees, combined with the delightful, often surprising, scents of Magnolia's sweet perfume, the tropical hint of Pawpaw blossoms, and the crisp, resinous aroma of Hemlock -Spruce, all conspire to entice humans to linger, to become one with nature, even for those merely on their way to work.

Repeat visitors are drawn to the area not only by the unending, year-round accessibility of the outdoorsiness, but also by a deeper, perhaps subconscious, intrigue. They've heard the rumors of untold scuttlebutt believed to exist in weathered walls of tattered row houses along the riverfront, and in aged, yet cozy homes seemingly stacked upon the incline of a hill guarded by the stoic presence of a large water tank. A silent sentry of sorts.

It's conceivable tourists or passersby could catch wind of an unsolved crime or the tantalizing possibility of a hidden, untapped trove of local lore, they might just settle in for a spell, linger close to the area, or find reasons to visit more often. The occasional flashy sparkle on the water's edge has caught many an eye, just as gold did to the diggers of yesteryear.

One of these historical contributors, which helped shape Glassport, was chartered in 1891 right here in town: The United States Glass Company, its sprawling complex was conveniently located alongside the winding Monongahela River along Seventh Street. The shimmering, colorful shards of glass are still found scattered throughout many parts of town, though abundantly along the river's edge, serve as a tangible reminder of how bustling and industrious Glassport was in its early days, and how it ultimately earned its evocative name.

Glassport officially became a municipality in 1902, years after the U.S. Glass Company was operating at full capacity, famously setting precedents for the burgeoning glass, steel, tool, coke, and gas industries. Glassport had transformed into a vital industrial borough, attracting factories of all sorts, primarily due to its advantageous inland river navigation access. At times, the river, teeming with barges and boats, seemed busier than the developing highways.

This countrywide company specialized in a diverse array of products, from the vibrant iridescence of carnival glass to elegant dinnerware and even delicate jewelry. Manufactured in molds and in every color imaginable, their primary focus of business in Glassport was pressed glass, providing an abundance of employment opportunities for both residents and those who commuted to the thriving borough.

However, in the mid-1900s, an unseasonal, violent tornado wreaked havoc on the USGC location, leaving a trail of devastation. Perched atop the main building was an eighty-foot water tower, crucial for cooling the intensely hot glass-burning furnaces. But on one fateful day, those working inside watched in horror as the immense structure tore through the roof with a deafening crash. Disoriented survivors were dumbfounded.

As the molten liquid within the damaged furnaces oozed out, it solidified into an estimated

250-ton mass of solid glass. It spread and hardened across the vast warehouse floor. The estimated 90-mile-per-hour winds of the F-3 tornado seemed to pick and choose which structures to obliterate and which to leave unscathed.

As the storm's hysteria degenerated, thousands of people flocked to the ravaged glass company site. Driven by a morbid curiosity, they just wanted a glimpse or a snapshot of the solidified mass of leftover liquid glass. To the dismay of the company's owners, the plant essentially died instantly. The costs of rebuilding such extensive damage proved insurmountable, and the once-thriving complex was ultimately abandoned. Hundreds of employees faced immediate dejection, left to grapple with the daunting question of how they would provide for their families in the wake of such sudden economic upheaval.

One can't help but wonder if the companies that acquired or purchased the glass patents and patterns were the only true beneficiaries of this tragedy. Could they have inadvertently coined the now-familiar phrase, "Depression Glass?"

The Earth Goddess' raw power danced destructively across the industrial sector, then turned to the other side of town to the Broadway Roller Rink on Ohio Avenue. Newsreels of the time reported there were cheerleaders inside, diligently practicing routines for upcoming competitions and crucial high school tryouts. Locals recounted how the wind ripped the roof off the building and caused walls to collapse, trapping the young athletes inside. Miraculously, none of them sustained serious injuries.

This seemed an apparent act of divine intervention, leaving many residents scratching their heads. Interestingly, the looming recession sat restlessly on the horizon. Years after the devastating tornado, the discovery of long-forgotten bank files revealed The United States Glass Company had engaged in numerous, and rather peculiar, contracts with companies seemingly unrelated to their core business practices, such as horse stables and garment factories.

Was the demise of this once prosperous, small -town cornerstone truly an unforeseen tragedy, or was the company's foundation already weakened by these odd financial entanglements?

Again, just another layer of the intriguing, and sometimes unsettling, oddity thickening the very air of Glassport.

Jittery Jody

Lucky breaks were something Lieutenant Kelly O'Malley often hoped for. He figured being Irish couldn't hurt — his four-leaf clover keychain was a constant companion, and his Saint Christopher medal swung faithfully from the rearview mirror of his police cruiser. So, locating Jody Larmi's home with relative ease felt like a promising start to his day.

His first interviewee resided in the Glassport Hill area. True to the region's gently meandering slopes, modest homes were scattered amongst the towering trees generously dotting the hillsides. Jody's residence was unassuming, functional rather than fancy.

As O'Malley approached the house, a woman emerged to meet him halfway down the walkway. Her sudden appearance startled him slightly as he expected to knock on the door.

"Oh, hi, are you Jody Larmi?" he asked, his voice calm despite the brief surprise.

"Yes, I am. And you are…?" Her tone held a hint of apprehension.

Flashing his worn badge, O'Malley introduced himself. "I'm Lieutenant Detective Kelly

O'Malley with the Glassport Police. I'm investigating a very old cold case murder of Karl Schmidt from 1970."

Jody's eyes widened slightly. "Wow, Detective, I was cleared of any wrong-doing years ago." Her voice trembled a little.

"Yes, I understand you were," O'Malley reassured her gently. "But I was hoping you'd be willing to go over the details again with me. Perhaps you could help me fill in some of the blanks. This case is new to me, and sometimes a fresh perspective, combined with the original details, can uncover overlooked clues. Would you mind telling me about your relationship with Karl? Maybe start from the beginning?"

Jody hesitated for a moment, her gaze drifting.

"It was so many years ago, but I can try." As they slowly walked towards her front door, she gestured towards a neighboring property.

"The house down there, near the old barn, is where he used to live. Our families often shared backyard barbecues back then. But Karl was involved in something truly awful with some young children near the creek, I think it was around 1945. For some dumb reason, he felt the need to brag about it to me, years later. He told me how he 'handled' it with his horse, boasting he could make any horse do anything he wanted." A shiver seemed to run through her.

"How did everyone else react to his bragging?" O'Malley asked, his tone carefully neutral.

"I guess he only ever bragged to me," Jody replied, her voice barely above a whisper.

"Why you, do you think?"

Her expression hardened slightly, a flicker of old anger in her eyes. "He was always trying to get in my pants, but I was only 14!"

O'Malley's eyebrows rose slightly. "So, did he?"

"Did he what?" Jody's voice was sharp, defensive.

"Did he get in your pants.?" O'Malley clarified gently.

"NO! Never! But he certainly tried."

O'Malley paused, letting the tension in the air settle for a moment. "So, Ms. Larmi, did you kill Karl Schmidt?"

"No, Sir. Our squabble happened in the summer of 1962. Back then, I was raising my beautiful twelve-year-old daughter as a single mother, and Karl couldn't keep his lecherous eyes off of her. At one of our afternoon picnic gatherings, he got a little too close to her for my liking. So I flat out yelled at him, right there in front of everyone:

'If my daughter is anywhere near the barbeque grill getting something to eat, then you'd better be over at the ice tub getting a beer. Make sure

you don't ever come near her or make any kind of move on her, or I WILL KILL YOU!'"

"Yes, I said it out loud, and I meant every word. Luckily, there were witnesses. They all knew what a disgusting creep he was, especially around cute, young girls. And yes," she added, "you know I was interrogated after he was killed. Detective, I passed a lie detector test because I was too dumb to know how to beat it. They believed my story back then, and they let me go. Until now?" Her eyes pleaded for reassurance.

O'Malley sighed softly, his gaze empathetic. "Jody, I believe you. But I needed to hear it from you directly. You're not dumb; you're honest. That's likely why you passed the test all those years ago. You're not under investigation now. I was just hoping you might recall some new, perhaps forgotten names or details from the past. I'm trying to figure out which direction to take this investigation, and where to look next. Would you be willing to show me the approximate area where this creek incident you mentioned occurred?"

"Yes, Detective, come this way." Jody started walking, a weariness in her steps. "After decades of working tables at the Cozy Cup coffee shop down near Perry and Pine Streets, I sometimes feel like a worn-out spring chicken, but I can still manage a walk over to the hillside."

Jody led O'Malley down a sloping hill overlooking a picturesque pasture where several horses grazed peacefully near a small creek meandering across the lower part of the hill. She pointed vaguely in the direction of where Karl had described his disgusting story.

"Detective O'Malley, please remember I wasn't actually there, but that's the general area Karl pointed out to me. The only ones who were there were those kids, and I don't recall any of them ever talking about it afterwards. Our neighbors' horses have always grazed peacefully in the pasture while drinking from the creek. The kids often waded through it, searching for those lucky pieces of colored glass or simply trying to cool off on a hot day. If the breeze was right, children from nearby streets would come to this hill to fly their kites. But Karl never liked seeing anyone having fun. He'd often bridle his horse, sometimes even riding bareback, and gallop as fast as he could back and forth across the hill, just to deliberately scare them. Karl described how he galloped his horse directly at those little kids. He burst out laughing as he recounted this horrid story. He said the kids were crying and yelling, begging him to stop as they tried to get out of the way, but the youngest and smallest ones were too slow. Karl bragged how they stumbled, so he just trampled right over them." Jody's voice was filled with a mixture of disgust and lingering horror.

"Jody, wow, that seems incredibly difficult to believe," O'Malley said, his brow furrowed in disbelief and concern.

"Karl told me as he jumped up onto that big boulder over there, proclaiming some kind of great victory. He had such a cruel streak. I've never understood why his parents never tried to correct his awful behavior. Maybe he bullied them too, or maybe they were just as mean-spirited."

"Thank you, Ms. Larmi," O'Malley said, his voice grave. "Even a disturbing visual of a past event can be helpful when investigating a murder, especially one as old as this. What about your daughter? Is there any possibility I could meet her? Is she still in town?"

Jody's face clouded with a sudden sadness. "Oh, my dear daughter, Aimee. I'm sorry, Detective, but I don't know where Aimee is now. She kind of disappeared years ago during her time in college. She was always obsessed with travel, probably because I kept her so close until college. I hope she'll come home one day. It's discouraging not knowing where she is." Her voice trailed off. "As for your interest in anyone else, well, like I said, I wasn't there and I'm afraid there may not be too many of us left in town to talk to. You have a difficult task ahead of you, Detective."

O'Malley nodded understandingly. "You mentioned Karl had a reputation for pursuing young girls. Do you recall any specific names of girls who may have been with him after you? There's some vague evidence suggesting he was involved with younger high school cheerleaders later in his life. Can't figure out how he attracted these gals."

Jody frowned, trying to recall details from so long ago. "I kinda remember a girl named Heidi Drew, but don't recall many specific names. But yes, back then, for many girls – and some boys, too – cheerleading wasn't just a school activity; it was a way of life. And for Glassport, it was more than just high school and college sports. It was a true statewide competitive tradition. Right here in Glassport, the annual cheer competition draws huge crowds from neighboring towns, counties, and even other states. You know," a wry smile touched her lips, "an event like that one probably made creepy Karl very happy."

Creek Catastrophe

Glassport Hill held a special magic for the local children. The air would often ring with their laughter, chuckles, and excited giggles as neighborhood kids raced up and down its dirt and paved roads, their colorful kites dancing against the blue sky, each trying to send their flyer higher than the rest. But on a warm, breezy day in May of 1945, the gentle late spring winds took a sudden, malevolent shift.

Innocent childhood merriment twisted abruptly into screams of terror and desperate cries as one of the older neighbor boys unexpectedly emerged from a barn at the bottom of the hill. He leaped onto his horse's bare back and deliberately spurred the animal to a gallop, racing directly toward the unsuspecting group of playful children.

It seemed his cruel focus was fixed on the smallest among them. The tiny caterwauler, startled and off-balance, tripped, slipped on the damp grass and rocks, tumbling into the shallow creek just as the young hooligan and his thundering horse bore down upon him. Matching the shrill cries of the terrified children, flocks of Common Grackles and iridescent Blue Jays erupted in shrieks as they exploded from the surrounding trees, a feathered echo of the chaos below.

As far as anyone ever knew, Karl Schmidt never once looked back to see if any of the children were seriously injured. He simply continued his reckless ride across the hillside, but it surely appeared the smallest one might be dead.

5 ~

Contemptible Karl

It was as if Karl Schmidt was a bad seed from the day he was born. He delighted in tormenting every kid he encountered, whether at school, on the street, or even in the bustling marketplace. Strangely, however, he seemed to possess a peculiar affinity for horses, a weird bond making many people wonder as contrary given the animals' typically intuitive and sensitive nature.

Perhaps they sensed a deep-seated thirst for calmness within him, a temporary respite from his inner turmoil, until he inevitably subjected them to his rough and often cruel handling. Even his own parents seemed distant and overwhelmed, merely trying to navigate their own difficult lives.

If someone, anyone – perhaps one of his teachers – could have recognized the talent flickering beneath his abrasive exterior, he might have been guided down a different path. Moreover, the pervasive anxieties and distractions of World War II cast a long shadow over everyone's lives, so it could be understandable, though no less tragic, his family and educators may have inadvertently turned a blind eye to his escalating issues.

One could only guess at the internal battles he faced, but the sheer energy and focused attention required to redirect a troubled child's path during such stressful times likely felt like an insurmountable task.

The boy possessed a raw, untapped potential, but only the school custodian, a quiet observer named Mr. Martin Everett, seemed to notice his handyman skills, though his initial motivation was simply to distract Karl away from his relentless bullying of the other kids.

One day, during the noisy chaos of lunchtime, Mr. Everett spotted Karl aiming a half-eaten apple at a small first grader, poised to launch his latest projectile.

"Karl," Mr. Everett called out, his voice firm but not unkind, "what in the world are you doing? Is there ever a single minute, hour, or day when you can just be civil to these other kids? We all have to share this space, and you seem determined to make life miserable for everyone."

Karl shrugged, a defiant glint in his young eyes. "Mr. Everett, I got ants in my pants, ya know? Gotta be doin' somethin' to make me laugh. And this stuff does it for me."

"But Karl," Mr. Everett persisted, his gaze steady, "you've got skills, real skills. I see it in the way you take things apart and sometimes even put them back together. Your brain is always ticking, I can tell. Why not work with me a few days a week?

I can teach you how to fix things properly, give you an outlet for all your energy, and maybe, just maybe you'll leave the other kids alone."

Karl's expression shifted from defiance to suspicion. "Like what? Mopping floors?"

Mr. Everett chuckled softly. "No, not just mopping. Fixing things around the school. Broken desks, wobbly shelves, leaky faucets. Sometimes I could really use an extra pair of hands. What do you think?" Mr. Everett extended a calloused hand towards the wary eighth grader.

Karl hesitated, then gave a small, almost imperceptible shrug before briefly shaking Mr. Everett's hand. "Okay, I guess we can try it a couple of times. But I'm not promising I'm gonna change."

"That's alright, Karl," Mr. Everett said, a flicker of hope in his eyes. "Meet me right here tomorrow after you finish eating lunch, and we'll tackle a squeaky door in the library. Deal?"

Mr. Everett was too young to have served in World War I and too old for active duty in World War II or the Korean War, but he firmly believed he was serving his country in his own way by keeping a watchful eye on the youth of Glassport. Having worked at the school for nearly fifteen years, he had witnessed countless students pass through its halls, but Karl was a stark anomaly, a truly radical exception. He held only a fragile hope he might exert some positive influence on this volatile young firecracker. Karl was already in eighth grade and would soon be heading to the less familiar territory of high school.

Intrigued and wanting to understand the roots of Karl's behavior, Mr. Everett discreetly checked with the principal to review Karl's school file. However, it contained little beyond a litany of his disruptive and often aggressive behavior within the school itself.

"You know, sir, child-rearing choices are a pervasive issue including a dysfunctional family and birth defects." Scowled Mr. Everett as he chatted with the principal. "Research shows victims of a hard-knock life often carry deep emotional scars, which can manifest in contemptible behavior. If Karl is mimicking actions he'd experienced, no one would ever know because we never discuss or deal with them."

The principal, a man weary from years of managing the daily dramas of adolescence, simply nodded, taking a quiet pride in his staff, knowing full well a caring and observant custodian like Mr. Everett was a rare and valuable asset to the school community.

6 ~

Perplexed Progress

"Whatcha got for me, O'Malley?" Captain Grey asked.

"Well, Jody Larmi tells me that jerk, Karl Schmidt, yes, I said jerk, may have been involved with several cheerleaders back in the day. She wasn't entirely sure, but the only name she could clearly recall was Heidi Drew. She believes Heidi would have been in high school around the mid-1950s. It might be worthwhile to look up information on as many cheerleaders from those years as possible, just in case there are other connections. Jody also mentioned the annual cheer competitions here; we might even extend our search beyond the county."

Captain Grey leaned back in his chair, a quizzical expression on his face. "Geez, K.O., I'd sure like to know Schmidt's secret. I was a decent guy in high school and didn't have nearly as much luck with the girls." He growled with a grin.

O'Malley settled at his own desk. "I'll start by digging through more high school records to pinpoint Heidi's graduation year and identify others who might have been in her class. I'm also wondering if any of them were involved in high school gangs, though those were relatively rare around here, weren't they? I'll do my best to uncover information about her life during and after high school. Someone out there must remember something."

"You know, K.O.," Captain Grey mused, "this might have been around the time folks were starting to migrate south from Pittsburgh, seeking a quieter lifestyle. There could have been individuals who weren't originally from Glassport involved in Schmidt's life. Just keep at your own steady pace, and we'll crack this darn thing."

With the other employees out for their lunch break, each was absorbed in contemplating their next investigative steps, but O'Malley decided to take a quick walk. He had always been captivated by the often-overlooked beauty of the Monongahela River, even though its name seemed to trip up almost everyone who tried to pronounce it. As much as he sometimes felt a pull to simply drift along with its swift current, he knew it wasn't an option at the moment. He just needed a dose of sunshine to re-energize him for the task ahead. He took a personal pride in solving cases, seeing them through to completion, so the fact this isolated one had gone cold so long ago was exceptionally frustrating. But a new idea was beginning to form in his mind, a spark of hope in the perplexing puzzle.

Back at the office, O'Malley began to assemble a working evidence bulletin board. He found an old rolling whiteboard and started taping up notes, timelines, and names. As a work in progress, a visual representation of their unfolding investigation. Grabbing a fresh cup of office coffee, he wheeled the board into Captain Grey's office. "Whatcha think, Captain?"

Captain Grey's eyes lit up as he surveyed the board. "Eureka, K.O.! This is a fantastic idea. It'll work great for us. And as it happens," he added, reaching for a file on his desk, "I already have some preliminary information on Heidi Drew to add to it. According to these old school records, she was in high school between 1952 and 1956. One of her classmates, who is now her husband, Wayne Healy, enlisted in the Army after college. After his retirement, he and Heidi moved back to Glassport, where he joined the fire department. It should be relatively easy to track them down through city records or the fire department roster. Let's see what they remember.

7 ~

Defiant Heidi Drew

O'Malley discovered the Healy couple had moved back to the Glassport Hill water tank area, too. This area was said to be a wonderful place for families and the best kite flying area because the gusts and gales would swoop up from the bottom of the hill, scoop the kites, and give the kids a staggering shuttle to brag about. After taking a gander at the flourishing wildflowers on the hill area where Karl supposedly lived, he then saw her house, walked up and knocked on the door. A woman answered.

"Hi, I'm Lt. Detective Kelly O'Malley of the Glassport Police Department and I'm investigating a cold case. Are you Heidi? I'm trying to find out who killed Karl Schmidt."

"Yes, I'm Heidi. Am I a suspect?"

"Heidi, you're not a suspect, but everybody who was associated with him back then is a person of interest. I recently learned while you were a high school cheerleader, and you had more than a casual relationship with Karl."

"Well, come in then, Lt., but you know, bad history never dies. This may take a while, so have a seat."

"Thanks. Can you tell me how you happened to get involved with an older guy?"

"Well, detective, I've always tried to keep up appearances. I even became a professional hairdresser after high school. As for Karl, he was always on the hunt for pretty girls. Hanging around at our basketball and football games, he'd appear in the bleachers out of nowhere and sit as close as he could to the cheerleaders, constantly ogling us."

"Well, you're still very attractive, so you must've been a beauty queen in high school. The boys had to have a hard time resisting you back then."

Heidi blushed a bit, amused she was still considered pretty at this age..

"I did make a big effort to look good in high school which did attract Karl."

"You'd think the school would've done something to keep us safe, especially since he was older, but they didn't. Because he was there spending lots of money, they didn't bother. Anyway, after one of the games, I was talking to my friend, another cheerleader. I told her if I had enough money, I'd buy this certain dress then maybe this guy, Brady would ask me to the prom. So, when everybody split for home, Karl was still there and must've overheard us talking. He whispered in a kinda creepy voice,

I'll buy that dress for you.

We both snickered at this older guy who was always chasing cheerleaders, but now he was sitting as close to me as he could. I was just a greedy kid and really wanted that dress.

Will you really get that dress for me? I asked. *Yes, anything for you,* Karl replied, smiling sheepishly.

So, he did get me the prettiest dress, but sadly, Brady and the prom never happened. Karl always had plenty of money, so he gave me other things like a nice watch, fancy jewelry and spending money. I was the best dressed girl in high school. All the attention was mesmerizing and addictive."

"But so far in our old reports, it doesn't say what kinds of jobs Karl held, so it doesn't seem he'd be good at earning money. Do you know how he'd earn it?"

"He was quite a few years older when I was in high school and boasted about his skills to handle and work with horses. He also told me he learned welding while in the Korean War and bragged about his SEABEE status, whatever that was. It didn't seem difficult for him to get a job with military grade welding skills. He said everybody needed a welder for something, especially down on the docks or the bridges. Those barges were coming and going all the time. If he would've just lived his life right, he'd still be here to brag about it, and you'd arrest him for all his foolishness. As for me, every boy in school tried to date me, but I would just slip away from all of them. I just wasn't ready to be tied down like the other girls. The boys thought it would be funny to nickname me *slippery slut.*"

"Heidi, that must've been so difficult for a teenager to deal with."

"Oh, Detective, it was embarrassing, but it only got worse. At football games, the cheerleaders would cheer, Go, Lions, go, Lions, go, Lions! But the boys in the stands cheered even louder, yelling,

Slippery slut, slippery slut, slippery slut!" Heidi just sighed.

"Some of our cheers also required the Cheer Squad boys to toss the girls up in the air and then catch us on our backs as we tossed our green and white pompoms into the air. But one day at school, another student named Wayne approached me after lunch and said he heard some of the guys talking about how they were going to purposely drop me. I really liked Wayne and considered him one of the good guys, so from then on, I didn't stay on my back but would land on my feet. I would stumble, but didn't get hurt. But because of my maneuver, I got thrown off the cheerleading squad even though I reported their nasty stunt to our Cheer Squad Leader. She wouldn't protect me from them. Anyway, Wayne & I became best friends and after high school, we eloped. Since Wayne was in R.O.T.C during high school and then college, he enlisted in the Army as an Officer and shipped out to Germany. He served for 20 years. After we came home, he joined the Glassport Fire Department."

"Wow. So, Heidi, do you own a gun?"

"No, Sir."

"How about Wayne?"

"Maybe. Because of his R.O.T.C. experience, he was immediately commissioned as Army 2nd Lieutenant, so probably had a gun. He went to Officer Candidate School or OCS, but I don't recall seeing a gun."

"Heidi, Karl Schmidt was killed on October 17th, 1970. Do you remember where you were?"

"As I said, Wayne shipped out to Germany for the Army and was still there during October 1970. I finished college in 1961 and joined him overseas."

"Heidi, this was truly enlightening. Kind of disheartening, but at least you survived. Thank you so much for your cooperation."

"I'm glad to help, Detective, but if you do anything to remind my husband, Wayne, of my *slippery slut* days, you will find me very hostile. I may be pretty, but I can become a raging bitch."

"I'll be very careful with this sensitive information and will only call you if I need anything more." O'Malley thanked Heidi and left.

8

More Mystery

Captain Grey summoned O'Malley to his office for an update. He opened his field report folder on Heidi and Wayne Healy.

"K.O., so you confirmed the whereabouts of Mr. and Mrs. Healy. I see they were in Germany the entire month of October 1970. Lt. Swanson, formerly in Narcotics, confirmed he served with Healy over there as well. In fact, Healy was stationed there for years."

"Yes, Heidi confirmed he was commissioned for 20 years. I think I told you she joined him after college. It feels good, early in this investigation, to move a few names to the positive side of our board. I do need to talk to Heidi again about other girls, like if she remembers Aimee Larmi, during her high school or college days. I'm hoping after our earlier chat, she remembered some names, but for now I'll let her be."

"Who's this Aimee Larmi?" Asked Grey.

"Just got wind of Jody having a daughter, but she didn't expand on her at all until I asked. You gotta pull this stuff out of these people. She did say Aimee disappeared years ago and has no idea of her whereabouts. I'll head back to Heidi's house in a bit.

Her feathers were ruffled, so hopefully she's settled down a bit."

9

Detect, Detective!

Heidi was diligently tending to her flourishing vegetable garden on the sunny side of her house when O'Malley's cruiser pulled up the driveway. The air was fragrant with the earthy scent of turned soil and the delicate perfume of blooming herbs.

"Hi, Mrs. Healy, I'm back," O'Malley said, stepping out of his car with a polite smile. "Both of your alibis have been checked out. Thank you again for the information you provided earlier. I was hoping our previous conversation might have jogged your memory about other details, especially concerning your high school years. Is there any chance you might recall some of the other girls Karl could have been involved with? Our initial inquiries suggest there were quite a few cheerleaders at Glassport High School and the surrounding area schools."

Heidi straightened up, wiping her gloved hands on her gardening apron. A thoughtful frown creased her brow. "I still honestly have no idea, Detective. It was such a long time ago, and after high school, it seemed like everyone scattered like dandelion seeds in the wind. Being finally free to pursue our own paths, like I did, our choices really depended on scholarships or our parents' financial means to further our education. Some went off to college, others to trade schools, or like me, followed their husbands overseas. Some talked about religious studies, but I really don't know. Maybe some became doctors or teachers. I truly wish I could offer you more concrete help, but you might be searching for ghosts. Karl, he pursued anyone who would give him the time of day, even a passing glance or a sharp word. He seemed to interpret every interaction as some sort of flirtation."

O'Malley shifted his weight. "Did Karl ever mention an incident involving him and some children at the creek near his family's farm? Did he ever name any of those kids? I'm really hoping to find one of them. Do you happen to remember a girl named Aimee Larmi?"

Heidi shook her head. "I can't help you with the creek incident, Detective, as I wasn't involved or aware of it at the time. Although there was a significant age difference between us, Aimee and I sometimes did homework together, either at her mother's coffee shop or at their house. But you're the detective, aren't you? Surely you can figure this out." There was a playful challenge in her tone.

"Yes, ma'am," O'Malley replied, a wry smile touching his lips. "I've been with the county Police Department for 2+ decades as a detective, but please understand, we'll take any credible tips we can get on cold cases like these. This one has so many unexpected twists and turns, so many dead ends and missing pieces in the file. It's truly flabbergasting."

Heidi leaned on her garden hoe, her gaze direct. "Well, duh, Mr. Detective Kelly O'Malley, detect."

With his metaphorical tail tucked firmly between his legs and a distinct feeling of being gently but firmly chastised, O'Malley retreated to his cruiser and drove away, perhaps a little faster than necessary. *Yikes. She's one scary broad when she wants to be,* he thought.

10 ~

Lieutenant Detective Kelly O'Malley

After a spicy yet insightful visit with Heidi Drew Healy, O'Malley decided to unwind with a beer at one of Glassport's quieter, classy watering holes, Cloak & Dagger Bar and Grill. Catching up with a few old friends from the force might offer a different perspective and help calm the lingering effects of his encounter with Heidi before he headed home to his wife of twenty-eight years, Norma Jean. Life had been good to them, even with his unpredictable schedule serving various precincts occasionally in need of extra investigative support.

As he nursed his beer and allowed his thoughts to drift back to the 1970 Schmidt murder, O'Malley recalled police activity had been extraordinarily hectic back then. He had just joined the force himself and was deeply involved in a complex case in McKeesport, a town just north and east of the confluence of the Monongahela and Youghiogheny rivers. Given his inexperience and the demands of the other investigation, it wasn't entirely far-fetched why this local case had completely slipped his radar.

A couple of familiar faces offered him a brief salute as they were leaving, but O'Malley remained at the bar, quietly pondering the day's frustrating lack of progress. However, a different, sad old case unexpectedly surfaced in his memory: one of Alfred McNeese. He valued Alfred's unique talent, as did almost every other resident of Glassport.

Although his life was as unassuming as the tiny, gray cobblestones of yesteryear, Alfred was a true master of his craft, one of the last great artists in his garment repair field. He was considered a quiet town hero for his impeccable shoe-stitching skills. Often the subject of local gossip, many residents felt his small, unassuming shop held a mysterious enigma. Regardless of the whispers and speculations, Alfred simply did his work, diligently, the best he could.

Back then, local kids joked his shop was haunted, their pinky-promises a testament to their unwavering belief he was some sort of benevolent wizard. And in a way, he was. He possessed an almost magical ability to repair every type of shoe with the most meticulous stitches and an extraordinary talent for mending the ravaged soles of even the most worn-out boots. It could certainly be considered a bewitching skill, even if his interpersonal skills were somewhat lacking and occasionally a little spooky.

Contradictory to his reserved personality, many customers held the opposite view when it came to his hands. Despite years of rigorous, often rough work, he possessed the most surprisingly tender touch. Whenever you picked up your repaired shoes or other leather goods, he always thanked you with a firm but gentle handshake, a stark contrast to the gritty reality of the world just beyond his shop's two tall, dust-streaked windows.

O'Malley vividly recalled one ordinary evening as Alfred was carefully locking up his shop.

There was some kind of event happening in town, which unfortunately drew several rough-and-tumble, less-than-welcomed visitors from the more rural northern counties, including a notorious motorcycle gang.

Right outside his shop, on the corner of Vermont Avenue, a wide sidewalk beckoned residents out for an evening stroll, and on warmer days, it often accommodated parents pushing baby strollers.

As Alfred turned the key in his lock, a deep, vibrating rumble grew rapidly louder, echoing down 8th Street from the direction of the river. Alfred frowned at the sudden intrusion of noise, picked up his worn leather satchel, and turned to walk towards his aging sedan parked across the street. As ill luck would have it, two of the motorcycles collided violently as they attempted to make the sharp turn onto Vermont. The heavy bikes skidded out of control, sliding across the wide sidewalk directly in Alfred's path.

Police sirens wailed in the distance, followed quickly by the flashing lights of ambulances, but they arrived too late to save Alfred. A palpable sadness hung heavy in the air of Glassport for days, weeks, and even years afterward, as they mourned the loss of a beloved member of their close-knit community, the only reliable shoe repairman for miles around. Flags were lowered to half-mast, and many residents grieved his passing more deeply than that of a close relative. Talented craftsmen like Alfred were becoming increasingly rare, and his death marked the beginning of the decline of one of those quietly essential lost arts. With the ensuing legal aftermath dragging on seemingly forever, Alfred's small shop stood empty and silent for years.

Once it was finally renovated and deemed ready for a new business to occupy the space, visitors to the location often swore it possessed a bewildering and unsettling aura, a lingering presence. Alfred's ghost, it seemed, wasn't quite ready to retire...alive or dead.

11 ~

Mobster Mastery

O'Malley jingled the loose change in his pocket nervously as he entered the bustling squad room, his footsteps led him directly to the familiar confines of the captain's office.

"Captain," he began, his voice tinged with frustration, "I've hit a wall with current suspects. I'm starting to feel like I'm chasing my own tail. Heidi Drew Healy provided very little concrete information about her high school classmates, saying they all went their separate ways after graduation, and she honestly couldn't recall who ended up where. Just making general guesses, she suggested some went to college, others learned a trade, some followed their husbands overseas like she did, and she even speculated a few might have entered religious orders, and maybe a handful became doctors or nurses." O'Malley sighed. "An era of so many possibilities."

Captain Grey gestured towards a chair. "Anything else of significance from your conversation with Mrs. Healy?"

O'Malley continued, "She's a bit...evasive, and I must keep reminding myself how much time has passed. Usually, cheerleaders are a close-knit group, almost like sisters, but I suppose we can't fault her for not remembering specific details. Heck, sometimes I can't even recall what we had for dinner last night. But after doing this for as long as I have, my gut tells me someone, somewhere, is deliberately withholding information. This definitely feels like a revenge killing or maybe I am getting too old for this kind of intricate game of hide and seek. I have a weird sense you might be holding something back, a bit of information you haven't shared with me yet. What gives, Captain?"

Captain Grey leaned forward, his expression serious. "Obviously, we chose the right guy to work this case. Okay, Kelly, you deserve God's honest truth here. It's unbelievable for our part of Pennsylvania, but Karl Schmidt was killed in a very specific way. I deliberately withheld this detail, hoping one of these potential suspects might inadvertently mention something about it, but sadly, it hasn't happened. His killing bears the hallmarks of a classic Mafia technique: the victim is first shot precisely in the heart, ensuring they live just long enough to see the gun barrel coming between their eyes. The Mafia refers to this grim method as 'H&H': Heart and Head. I apologize for the cloak and dagger, but your instincts are correct; it strongly suggests a planned revenge." Grey tapped his pen on his desk, his gaze unwavering.

"Holy shit," O'Malley exclaimed, his eyes wide with surprise. "Now that's a real humdinger.

But here in Glassport? Has there ever been a significant Mafia influence here? Do you think Karl somehow got tangled with a Mafia-related cheerleader or someone connected to the mob world? This seems like such a small, relatively quiet place for that kind of activity. Holy smokes, Captain, that's a massive detail to leave out. This needs to be kept under wraps until we reach a conclusion, hopefully sooner rather than later. Thanks for finally letting me in on this gem. It gives me a totally different perspective and a massive shift in the vibe of this case."

"Again, my apologies for not being forthcoming with you from the beginning, Kelly, but I genuinely hoped we'd hear something corroborating this detail from a suspect," Captain Grey said, a hint of regret in his voice as he waved O'Malley towards the door.

Yelling back over his shoulder as he headed out of the office, O'Malley said, "Since our list of viable suspects isn't exactly growing at the moment, I'll ask my wife's second cousin if she can do a deep dive into old local stories at the county library. Perhaps one of the kids involved in the creek incident won an award or rescued a cat from a tree or something to warrant their name in the newspaper. It'll be slow going, as those years of archived papers are likely still in hard copies or possibly microfiche. Whoever committed this crime has kept it remarkably close to the vest, Sir."

"K.O., also keep in mind those children would have been born somewhere in the late 1930s, so, yikes, they'd be close to sixty-five or seventy years old by now. I'll check with the County Tax Department; they might be able to help us determine if any of them are or were homeowners in the area. Finding individuals who may have lived in the Glassport Hill area around the October 1970 timeframe is vital. And let's not forget, O'Malley, during World War II, all the elementary-aged kids in town attended the same grade school downtown; it housed grades one through eight before they moved on to high school. Some of them must still be alive. Have you found anything relevant in the obituaries, possibly?"

"No, Sir, not yet, but if you've got the county property tax rolls covered, I'll check the school archives, comb through the library's newspaper archives, and take another, even closer look at the obituaries. We have to find someone, dead or alive, who can shed some light on this."

12 ~

Reliable Results

The rain continued its relentless descent as O'Malley, coffee cup warming his hands, stared out at the blurred world from his second-story office window. The raindrops, like miniature racers, competed for the quickest journey to the sill, carving tiny, temporary rivers down the aged, etched glass panes. Outside, a small flock of pigeons sought shelter, their plump bodies tucked into the narrow crevices of the exterior's aging stonework window trim.

Twenty-five years. A quarter of a century he'd dedicated to the county's detective division, serving in numerous stations, witnessing the spectrum of human behavior from the mundane to the monstrous. The ice-cold beer with the guys the other night had been a welcome respite, but the details of the decades-old Mob-style killing gnawed at him. How could such a brutal case, especially one involving children, have gone cold for so long?

Despite the fact it hadn't been his case initially, a deep unease had settled within him, an emotional tug he hadn't experienced in all his years on the force. *Shake it off,* he mentally commanded himself, taking a larger sip of his lukewarm coffee.

His desk was a landscape of his current preoccupation: scattered suspect files, a small collection of used coffee cups forming a brown ring on the worn surface, and the forlorn half-eaten donut, a testament to hours of distracted contemplation. The office was mostly deserted, the rhythmic tick of the wall clock amplified in the semi-quiet room, punctuated by the irritating, intermittent flicker of the blush-toned fluorescent lights overhead. The flickering was beginning to grate on his nerves; perhaps it was a sign to call it a day. He decided on one final check-in with Captain Grey, knocking softly on his office door.

"Captain, do you have anything else for me before I head home?"

Captain Grey looked up from a stack of papers, his expression thoughtful. "Yes, I believe so. Out of all the children who resided on or near Glassport Hill back in 1945, I've managed to locate two who are still alive and, remarkably, still living here in town. Their names are Marilu Grace and Scott Rand. Get a fresh start tomorrow, Kelly, and track them down. See what memories they hold, what they might be able to tell you. Good luck."

A surge of anticipation coursed through O'Malley. He hoped fervently these two-living links to the past could finally shed some much-needed light on the long shadows of this dark case.

13 ~

Gracious Marilu Grace

The morning sun, a pale gold, finally managed to pierce through the lingering westerly clouds as O'Malley arrived at the office. Thanks to Captain Grey for his diligent search of the databases of the department and the city for the most current contact information, he finally found addresses for both Ms. Grace and Mr. Rand. Grey handed the slip of paper to O'Malley who finally had a renewed sense of purpose after the potential breakthrough. O'Malley drove first to Marilu's house, located on a quiet street where Hemlock Way intersected with 9th. He parked at the end of the gravel driveway and walked towards the welcoming front door, knocking firmly.

"Hello, Marilu Grace? I'm Lieutenant Detective Kelly O'Malley with the Glassport Police, and I'm investigating a cold case incident from 1945."

A kind-faced woman with silver strands woven through her dark hair opened the door, her expression a mixture of surprise and gentle curiosity. "Yes, I'm Marilu. Oh, my golly, 1945... that was so long ago. I just made a fresh pot of coffee, Detective, won't you come in? I'm not sure I can be of much help with anything from that long ago."

O'Malley stepped into the cozy, slightly cluttered living room. "Thank you, Ms. Grace. This case involved a young Karl Schmidt and a group of children down by the creek in the Glassport Hill area. You and Mr. Scott Rand are the only individuals still residing in town I've been able to locate who might remember something. Can you recall any of the other children's names or any other details in your age group? Anything at all that rings a bell would be incredibly helpful."

Marilu gestured towards a well-worn armchair. "Cream for your coffee, Detective? I remember Scott Rand very well. He was younger than the rest of us and could be quite a little rascal back then. All the kids who lived up on Glassport Hill had to walk down the steep slope to school and then trudge back up every day to get home. He was always running at top speed, and my friend and I would often tease him about always wanting to be the first one to reach his house. But then he started grabbing our school papers and folders and deliberately throwing them on the ground."

"Yes, please, just a little cream would be perfect," O'Malley replied, accepting the offered mug.

Marilu poured the cream and continued, her gaze softening with the recollection. "My parents eventually complained about his behavior to the school and to his parents. I believe his punishment was to be kept after school for longer than the rest of us. When his detention ended, he was usually released at the same time as us, but thankfully, he didn't bother us anymore. He still ran incredibly fast and was invariably the first one to reach the top of the hill. Some of the houses up there had front concrete stairs, and he always bounded up them, never taking just one step at a time. But then one day, I remember seeing him looking very pale and walking with a noticeable limp. My friend and I were puzzled, so we asked him, 'Why so slow today, Speed Demon?'"

Marilu paused, a cloud shadow crossing her. "Scott responded, his voice quiet and serious for a little kid, 'My back hurts. Karl ran his horse over me.'"

She shook her head slowly. "We didn't question it at the time, which we probably should have, considering Karl was a very mean and nasty boy, and Scott was such a small, vulnerable kid. For such a small neighborhood, we really should have looked out for one another more."

Lieutenant O'Malley leaned forward slightly, his interest piqued. "Did you believe him, Ms. Grace? Can you tell me anything more about the incident? Any idea who the other children were playing by the creek?"

Marilu put a delicate finger to her lip, her eyes scanning the room as if searching for long-lost memories in the dust motes dancing in the sunlight. "Scott did have a brother who was one grade ahead of him in school, and I believe there was also an older cousin who sometimes played with them. I can't recall their names with any certainty now, but they might be able to offer some more information, if they are still living in the area. Here's my email address and phone number, Detective, if you have any other questions for me. It was nice to meet you."

"Thank you very much, Marilu. Just one more quick question, if you don't mind. What did you do after you finished high school? Did you go on to college? I didn't mean to sound nosy, just trying to connect as many dots as possible. I think we might finally be making some progress in this case."

Marilu offered a gentle smile. "No college for me, Detective. My parents weren't what you'd call well-to-do. My mother cleaned houses to make ends meet, so I followed in her footsteps. It was hard work, but it paid the bills for me and helped keep our small family farm afloat. We raised chickens and sold their eggs. It kept us going. Have a nice day, Lieutenant O'Malley." Marilu waved goodbye from her porch. "I'll certainly try to remember, though I can't promise anything."

Rand's Remarkable Rant

O'Malley felt a renewed sense of energy coursing through him as he headed toward Scott Rand's address. He was determined to finally reach the truth at the heart of this decades-old case. He briefly considered phoning ahead, but he had learned over the years that observing a person's initial, unguarded facial reactions upon his unexpected arrival often revealed more than a prearranged phone call ever could. These individuals were strangers to him, and he to them, so their inherent suspicion when he explained his presence was understandable, even warranted.

He arrived at the Rand residence, a modest house situated midway up Glassport Hill. He approached the paint-peeling front door of the somewhat dilapidated home, its state of disrepair suggesting upkeep was not a current priority. Just as he raised his hand to knock again, a gruff voice called out from the side yard.

"Hey, who are you?"

O'Malley rounded the corner of the house to find an older man with a weathered face and wary eyes tending to a small, overgrown vegetable patch. "I am Lieutenant Detective Kelly O'Malley of the

Glassport Police Department. I'm investigating the 1970 murder of Karl Schmidt. Is it true Karl Schmidt ran you over with his horse when you were a child?"

The man's eyes narrowed further. "Yes, sir, it damn well really happened. I was only six and a half years old at the time. My eight-year-old brother and older cousin were with me. It was supposed to be a fun day for us kids. This might seem irrelevant now, but for some damn reason, my mom made me wear long johns under my Levis, even though it was late May and getting warm. I was the slowest getting dressed in all those layers. After breakfast, we all went down to the creek to play, fly our kites, and skip rocks, but then Karl Schmidt showed up. He was the most spiteful kid in the whole damn neighborhood. He'd appear in the weirdest places at the weirdest times just to frighten us. He was older and could ride a horse real good. From down near the barn, we saw him bridle his horse, jump on its back bareback, and yell, 'Giddyap.' He headed straight for us, but made a fast pass, just close enough to really scare the living daylights out of all of us."

Scott was breathing heavily now, the decades -old memory clearly stirring up intense emotions.

"Take a breath, Scott. Here, have some water." O'Malley, sensing distress, retrieved a glass of water from Scott's kitchen.

Scott took a few shaky breaths and continued, his voice thick with resentment. "Then he turned his horse and rode in a wide half-circle. We heard him command his horse to charge towards us again. As the youngest, and sadly, the one dressed in heavy, wet jeans and those stupid long johns, I seemed to be his prime target. I stumbled on the slippery creek boulders and rocks as he galloped right at me. I had no time to protect myself as he bore down on me. The horse... the hooves... they pounded right into my lower back." Scott rubbed his lower back, a visible wince of pain crossing his face. "I never did a thing to Karl."

He paused, his voice dropping to a near whisper. "I've had back problems my whole life and the pain the horse inflicted on me was unforgettable. I still don't understand why it didn't break my back bones, but maybe those stupid thick long johns possibly saved me from being completely paralyzed. In my forties, I had a lumbar-sacrum strain, and the pain was identical. It's an unforgettable pain, Detective, nothing else has ever felt quite like it. As I said, my back problems have lasted a lifetime. Plus," his voice grew bitter, "this injury forced me to leave the Army early. I got an honorable discharge and came back home to work with my father in his lawnmower repair shop down on Broadway Street and Ohio Avenue. It kept us both busy, so maybe I was meant to be here with him. I may not be able to prove it now, but I place all the blame for my back problems on Karl for his stupid, childish, and dangerous tricks. He tormented us kids for years."

"Sounds like a powerful motive for revenge, Scott. Do you currently own a gun?" O'Malley asked, his tone carefully neutral.

Scott's gaze hardened. "I do. It's right here on the table."

"Have you fired it recently, Scott?" O'Malley pressed.

"No, not since I killed Karl." The words hung heavy in the air, the casual admission sending a jolt through O'Malley.

"What?" O'Malley gasped.

Scott shrugged, his expression a strange mix of defiance and resignation. "Look, Detective, I'm an old man now. I don't give a damn who knows. I just walked up behind him one day and put a bullet right through the back of his damn head. So, you wanna send me to prison? I'm ready. Okay, yes, prison. A bed. Three meals a day. Free medical. Sign me up."

"Wow, Scott," O'Malley said, his mind reeling from the unexpected confession. "I'm shocked you've held it in all these years. You never told anyone? You know, Scott, I have to take you in. After we book you, Captain Lance Grey will handle the interrogation. Then we'll let the District Attorney deal with the details. Give me your gun, Scott. I'll have to get it tested."

With a sigh of what seemed like both relief and weary acceptance, Scott nodded. O'Malley carefully cuffed Scott and put him in the back seat of the cruiser, the rain-soaked streets suddenly seeming to reflect the weight of the bygone secret finally brought to light.

15 ~

Ambiguous Obstruction

Without hurry, O'Malley drove back to the station. He then took Scott up to Captain Grey's office.

"Mr. Rand, I'm Captain Lance Grey. Lt. Detective Kelly O'Malley says you're going to tell us about this killing a childhood bully, Karl Schmidt."

"Like I told your Lieutenant earlier, I just walked up behind him in his barn and put a bullet through the back of his head."

Captain Grey frowned, and said, "Were there any witnesses?"

"No, I made sure."

"So, when did you do it?"

"It was summertime in 1970. I hated him for what he did to all of us kids, but mainly what he did to me. He used to say, *'a good horse is worth more than any two-legged human.'* What a jerk. Should've done it sooner."

Grey and O'Malley stepped outside the interrogation room to chat. Captain sighs and looks at the ceiling, "This case is really taking a toll on both of us and as much as I'd like to let Scott Rand take the fall, it sounds like we're getting an exaggerated misconception of a crucial event just for the peace of mind and security for the rest of his life."

O'Malley jingles the metal 4-leaf clover keychain in his pocket and blurts, "So, he's a liar. He's a bamboozler. You and I both know it. His home is in shambles, so admitting to the murder and going to prison probably looks like a sweet deal."

Both men return to the room and O'Malley says, "Ok, Mr. Rand, sit tight until the District Attorney decides what to do with you. One of the jailers will take you to booking and then you'll be in our temporary lockup for now."

They decided to let him incubate in the clink overnight giving Scott some time to think or sleep on his theatrics. Maybe, just maybe this overnighter would give him a taste of what he seems to want for the rest of his life and maybe force him to rethink this nonsensical admission.

16

Confession and Consequences

The following day, after a somewhat heated meeting with the District Attorney, Captain Grey and Lieutenant O'Malley returned to the secure jail area to have another conversation with Scott Rand.

"Mr. Rand," O'Malley began, his voice firm, "there are several significant discrepancies in your confession. First and foremost, our Ballistics specialists have determined the gun you claim to have used is not a match for the murder weapon. Second, Karl Schmidt was not killed on the date you claim to have murdered him. And third, you stated you shot him in the back of the head, but the autopsy report clearly indicates he wasn't shot in that part of his body." O'Malley laid out the facts.

Captain Grey followed up, his expression stern. "Do you honestly believe you can simply confess to a murder to live out the rest of your days in prison? Is this truly the best option you envision for the remainder of your life? Do you have any understanding of what obstruction of justice entails? Intentionally misleading a criminal investigation is a serious crime, Mr. Rand. We are leaving you here until the D.A. decides on how to proceed with you. Whether you realize it or not, your false confession has only created more chaos and wasted valuable time in our cold case investigation."

Scott Rand looked visibly disgruntled, his earlier bravado fading, but he knew they had caught him in his lie. He remained silent, awaiting their next move.

One of the towering jailers secured Scott's cell door with a loud clang as Captain Grey shot a disapproving look at Scott before exiting the area.

"K.O., I knew he was lying the moment he said he shot Karl in the back of the head," Captain Grey said, shaking his head. "I was just letting him dig himself into an even deeper hole. What are your thoughts now?"

"Just leave it for now," O'Malley suggested, his mind still grappling with the implications of the Mafia connection. "You mentioned the Mafia Technique, Captain. Do we really think there was Mob involvement in our little town? Karl Schmidt was a welder, though, not exactly a typical Mob target. I'm not sure what else he might have been involved in besides chasing young girls. Gambling? Running off his mouth to the wrong people? What would the Mob want with a small-town welder like Schmidt? Sorry, but my brain is just spinning in bizarre directions."

"I don't know, Kelly. The D.A. said we can address the obstruction issue as needed. In the meantime, perhaps another night in the Glassport

Police Department's less-than-luxurious accommodations will prompt Scott Rand to have a change of heart."

68

17

Life Lottery

Trying another shot at the truth, Captain Grey and Lt. O'Malley had the jailers bring Scott Rand into the interrogation room.

"You can't lie about a crime and think your life would be easier living in jail. We understand your struggles, and the mayor also sympathizes with you for the abuse you suffered at such a young age. I'm kind of embarrassed this case wasn't resolved back then, and some sort of compensation given to you from whatever property Karl had. Low back injury pain, like what you endured, does last a lifetime. You had the most knowledge of the whole mess, so we all do thank you for the gruesome details. I would rather be convicting Karl for the chaos he inflicted on you kids back then, but for now, Mr. Rand, you got lucky. No charges will be filed against you for obstruction or your imaginative scenario. The mayor is very grateful to you and the other victims of Karl Schmidt for exposing his true character. We're much more satisfied you aren't the killer."

Scott perked up and offered, "I can give you the name of another girl to look at. You know about slippery slut?"

"Yes, we cleared Heidi Drew," said Captain Grey. "But what do you know about her?"

"You both know I really wanted to kill Karl, so I would follow him often from place to place. One day, I saw slippery slut, sorry, Heidi Drew, get really mad at Karl. She was yelling and screaming at Karl because she found out another cheerleader was flirting with him. Right there, this other girl looked right at Karl and smiled as she posed seductively. That disgusting skunk moved right in leaving Heidi in the dust. She was topsy-turvy, upset like a rabid animal. I felt bad for her."

"You're telling us a young girl was chasing a creep like Karl Schmidt? Wow, what a switch. If any of these details end up helping us in some way, we may offer you a reward. A big maybe, though." Captain Grey was spent.

"Yes, Sir. I only know her name was Heather. After she got together with Karl, the boys at school nicknamed her Heather Honey."

"Scott, this better not be another fabrication. Just Heather, no last name? We'll put her on our persons of interest list and dig up some history. You can go now, Scott. We'll be in touch soon. Jailer, please take Mr. Rand to the desk Sergeant for processing his release." O'Malley instructed.

"Thank you, Scott. I want no more nonsense from you, or I will come down on you hard. Now git outta here." Frazzled, Captain Grey laced his fingers and stretched his hands over his head with an oversized yawn.

O'Malley grabbed the file folder, "I will investigate Heather Honey's history and status. A last name will get me a bit further, so I'll get moving on this."

18

Hunting for Heather Honey

Captain Grey leaned over O'Malley's desk, pointing at a printout. "I managed to track down our Heather Honey. Her current last name is Carmichael, and she lives in Port Vue. I've also got a local address and phone number here. Married a fellow named Jack, lives near the Youghiogheny River."

"Hey, Captain, want me to grab you a sandwich on my way back? My treat."

"Yeah, anything works, K.O."

"So, a chocolate chip pancake and egg sandwich?" O'Malley grinned, a playful glint in his eye.

As he walked toward his office door, Captain Grey tossed a crumpled piece of paper that bounced harmlessly off O'Malley's shoulder, with a soft chuckle. They were a good team.

With the new information clutched in his hand, O'Malley drove through the familiar streets, heading towards Port Vue and the home of Heather Houston Carmichael, formerly known as Heather Honey. He parked his cruiser, walked up the sidewalk, and knocked on the front door.

The door creaked open, revealing a man with a cautious expression. "Hi, who are you?"

Flashing his badge, O'Malley introduced himself. "I'm Lieutenant Kelly O'Malley, and I'm working on a cold case. Is Heather Carmichael home, by chance?"

"I'm her husband, Jack. What do you want with her?" Jack's tone was guarded.

From just behind the door, a woman's voice interrupted. "I overheard that. I'm Heather. Am I a suspect, Lieutenant?"

"Heather, if you knew Karl Schmidt, you're considered a person of interest in our investigation. May I come in? I'd appreciate it if you could tell me about your connection with Karl."

"Sure, come in. I'm sorry, hearing his name just shocked me. I haven't heard it in so long." Heather stepped into view, her expression a mix of surprise and a hint of unease. "Yes, I'll admit it. I was young and foolish, and I wanted the attention Karl gave Heidi. Yes, I felt guilty about it, well, seducing him. Karl gave me everything I asked for – trinkets, money – but then he started wanting more from me than I was willing to give, so I broke it off. He was violently angry about it. I remember one afternoon at a football game, he showed up and grabbed my arm. He was scolding me for being so ungrateful, but he picked the absolute wrong day to get rough with me because all my friends saw him, and my father was also at the game. He completely panicked when he saw this older guy yelling at me, and well, my father kicked Karl's ass."

"So, he gave him a bloody nose or a black eye, something painful?" O'Malley inquired.

Heather's expression was grim. "And a lot more than he expected, Lieutenant. His nose was gushing blood, and after my father was done with him, his face looked like raw hamburger. My father also broke Karl's arm, so crawling away was very difficult for him."

"Heather, did Karl ever press charges against your father for assault?" O'Malley asked, his eyebrows raised.

Heather scoffed. "And tell the police what? 'I was trying to get with a young girl, so her father beat me up?' I don't think so."

"Do you own a gun, Heather?"

Jack answered for her. "There's an old one in the closet, but we've never had any reason to use it. My father inherited it from my grandpa, but he passed away about thirty years ago."

"I'd like to speak with your father about it, if possible," O'Malley said, his gaze shifting to Jack.

"Lieutenant O'Malley, you're in luck. He'll be here in a few minutes for lunch."

Right on cue, a gentleman arrived at the door, and Jack introduced him as Mr. Walker Carmichael.

"Mr. Carmichael, I'm Lieutenant O'Malley from the Glassport Police Department. I apologize for interrupting your plans, but could you tell me a bit about your father's gun?"

Mr. Carmichael nodded. "Well, Lieutenant, my father brought it back from Italy after the war. As far as I know, it hasn't been used at all since then."

"Mr. Carmichael, with your permission, would it be possible for me to take the gun back to headquarters? I'd prefer to avoid getting a court order if possible. I can give you a receipt today. I'd like our ballistics team to check it out, both for your peace of mind and ours. Karl Schmidt was killed on October 17, 1970. Please take a moment to think about where you were. Your alibis would be greatly appreciated so I can clear you and your family. Let me know when you're ready, and we can arrange a meeting. I'll let Captain Grey know you're all willing to come to the station, correct?"

The three Carmichaels nodded their agreement.

O'Malley left and headed to the deli to pick up lunch. Upon his return to the station, he carefully balanced his briefcase and the sandwiches as the aroma of the pastrami wafted through the offices racing him to Captain Lance Grey's office. Grey was already smiling.

Pessimistic Positives

Heather, Jack, and his father, Walker, were composed and ready when O'Malley and Captain Grey greeted them at headquarters for their interview.

"Hello, everyone. I'm Captain Lance Grey." Offered with a polite nod. "We sincerely appreciate you agreeing to Lieutenant O'Malley's request to come in today so we can account for all individuals who had a connection with Mr. Schmidt. As you understand, anyone associated with Karl Schmidt remains a person of interest in this ongoing investigation. We are particularly interested in your father's gun, Mr. Carmichael. Oddly, our ballistics team has confirmed your firearm is indeed the murder weapon. However," Captain Grey paused, his expression puzzled, "there were absolutely no fingerprints found on it. None. Do you all have verifiable alibis for October 17, 1970?"

"What? How?" Mr. Carmichael exclaimed, his brow furrowed in disbelief.

"That's shocking to hear, but yes, sir, we do have solid alibis," Heather offered quickly. "We were all together at a Washington and Jefferson College football game in Waynesburg,

Pennsylvania. Jack and I are alumni, so we tried to attend as many games as possible, especially when they were playing a major rival. I was a cheerleader back then, and Jack was a linebacker. W&J was playing the Waynesburg Yellow Jackets."

"Walker, do you corroborate your children's statements?" O'Malley asked, his gaze steady.

"Yes, Lieutenant, I do. But I am utterly appalled about the gun. It stays hidden away, and none of us have ever had any reason to use it," he replied, his voice troubled.

Jack added, "After the game, my father and I were, well, goofing around and wrestling, you know how guys are, we never really grew up. Dad ended up hurting his ribs, so we thought it best to get it checked out at the university's clinic. Their records should reflect the incident if they still have them. Will it clear us in your eyes, Lieutenant?"

"As clear as day, as long as all details are as you've reported. If you happen to recall any further details, please don't hesitate to contact us. But for now, we'll need to delve deeper into the history of your gun, Mr. Carmichael. Walker, if you feel the need to discuss this further, please come in anytime so we can hopefully exonerate you and your family," Captain Grey said, concluding the interview. He thanked the family for their cooperation and led them towards the door.

20 ~

Convoluted Cliffhanger

The Pennsylvania drizzle was intermittent, but today it blurred the cheerful neon sign outside the small roadside cafe. Or were those happy tears clouding Aimee Larmi's view? Just two days ago, Aimee had been living a predictable life as a college student at Washington and Jefferson, but a restless yearning for adventure had taken hold. A rebel at heart, always had been, she hadn't even told her mother she was leaving.

She'd hitchhiked this far, fully aware of the inherent risks, intending to catch the first bus heading anywhere. She'd stopped at this quiet diner, needing a bite to eat and a moment to gather her thoughts. The only sounds were the melancholic hum of the jukebox, appropriately playing "Raindrops Keep Fallin' on My Head," and the occasional clatter of dishes from the kitchen. Aimee kept the hood of her sweatshirt pulled up, her head down, her eyes darting nervously towards the entrance every time the bell above the door chimed. She didn't want to run into anyone from school or the dorms. She needed to formulate a solid plan, and she wasn't ready to answer any questions about her impulsive, devil-may-care quest.

"Need a coffee refill, hon?" asked the friendly, curly-blonde-haired waitress.

"No, thank you," Aimee mumbled, avoiding eye contact.

"You from around here? You look kinda familiar," the waitress said, her eyes narrowing slightly as she turned to serve another customer.

Aimee reached into her worn backpack and pulled out a crumpled map of northwestern Pennsylvania. Her finger traced the winding roads, the names of small, unfamiliar towns, and the vast expanses of forests. Somewhere out there, she could disappear for a while, explore without the suffocating constraints of her mother's overprotective nature. She knew little of this part of the state; her mother had sheltered her fiercely, insisting on strict Catholic schooling and keeping a vigilant eye on her every move as she grew up.

She was miles away from her starting point and exhausted, but she needed to find a safe place to sleep. Before venturing out again, she bought a few basic supplies and some warm socks at the small market adjoining the coffee shop and then began her trek into the darkening woods, determined to make a plan for the following day.

The next morning, Aimee woke up in a relatively drier patch of the forest, although the air was thick with the earthy scent of pine needles and damp soil. The trees looked different in the soft morning light compared to the ghostly shadows of dusk when she had settled in for the night. Incredibly tall and imposing, their dark trunks skinnied as they reached towards the sky. She felt a strange, yet peaceful sense of protection beneath their skeletal-like finger branches that twisted and intertwined above her.

For today, she would avoid most of the main roads, the quieter backroads were somewhat safer in the daylight. After a few hours of walking, she passed several dilapidated, abandoned cabins, but none felt right. Similar to a Goldilocks moment, she had choices. Good? Bad? Up ahead, she spotted a small, cozy-looking cottage with a thin plume of smoke curling lazily from its chimney. Someone had to be there, but she hesitated to approach too closely. People living in the woods often owned guns for protection which made her more cautious. The front door, old and creaky, opened slowly just before she could bring herself to knock.

"You lost?" a rough-voiced old man asked, his eyes scrutinizing her.

"Hi, no, sir," she replied quietly, trying to sound less nervous than she felt. "I'm on an adventure, and I just need a place to stay for a day or two."

The old man studied her for a long moment, his gaze unwavering, before finally stepping aside, gesturing for her to enter. "Well, come on in then. My place is small, but it's cozy and safe enough.

Always got a fire crackling in the hearth. I enjoy watching the flames flicker on the walls, and the warmth keeps the dampness out." He introduced himself as Clarence, a retired logger who had lived in the solitude of the forest for years. Aimee hesitated, not yet ready to reveal her name. "Need something to eat, child?"

Over the next few days, Aimee found herself helping Clarence with simple chores: fetching water from a nearby stream, tending to a tiny, struggling garden he coaxed with the filtered forest sunlight, and surprising herself with a knack for chopping wood. In return for her help, he offered her hearty meals and a safe, quiet corner to sleep in each night.

After a simple dinner one evening, Clarence's weathered gaze turned thoughtful. "You running from something, girl?" he asked, his voice gentle but direct.

Aimee stiffened slightly, her heart skipping a beat. "What makes you say that, Clarence?"

"You got a look about you, like you're always listening for footsteps." His eyes held a knowing quality.

Aimee hesitated, then sighed. "It's complicated. But for now, I don't really have a choice."

"There's always a choice, child, you chose to stop here." Clarence said quietly, his gaze steady.

Aimee knew it was time to move on. She was starting to feel too comfortable in the old man's peaceful cottage, but she also didn't want to inadvertently put him in a difficult position if her mother started looking for her. When the sun finally broke through the trees the next morning, her few belongings were packed. She thanked Clarence with a heartfelt handshake and then a warm hug, before stepping back out through the same old, creaky door.

Clarence pressed a few crumpled bills into her hand and gave her an old map. It was much easier to read than her own. Now, she needed to decide which direction to take. She chose north. There were plenty of backroads to navigate, but time, she vaguely realized, was slipping away. After an hour or so, she stopped at another small, mom and pop shop. She gathered a few more food items and more clean socks and then noticed a sign for a commuter bus. Since she had made it north to Cranberry Township, she asked the elderly man behind the counter if this bus could take her further north. He nodded, so she bought a ticket and waited anxiously.

"Hey, Miss, the bus should be arriving any minute now," said a very sweet voice on the other end of the counter. It was a tiny lady with a nice smile. "Not sure how far you're going, but here's some homemade cookies for the trip. You be safe now."

Aimee's eyes brightened. She thanked the woman as the bus rumbled to a stop outside. She was the only one boarding at this stop, but several passengers were already settled in their seats. She found an empty seat in the very back and huddled down, her risky saga finally catching up with her. Still a kid in many ways, she hadn't fully considered the mental stress this impulsive, completely unplanned expedition would have on her. But for now, with the drizzling rain against the windows, all she craved was sleep. Using her small bag as a makeshift pillow, she laid across the seat, hoping the bus wasn't too bumpy.

Before she completely drifted off, she vaguely heard the bus driver announce they were heading up Highway 79. If her hazy recollection of the map was even remotely correct, they would be passing through Portersville. Anything to get further away from her old life.

She was suddenly jolted awake by the screeching of the bus brakes as it pulled to an abrupt stop. It was dark outside, and she felt completely disoriented. She could feel the dampness in the air and vaguely smelled water, wondering which river they might be nearby. Not a river, she realized seeing highway markers it was Lake Erie. A sudden rush of exhilaration coursed through her. She had never been this far away from home, never even seen any of the Great Lakes. She got off the bus, rubbed her tired eyes, and looked around at her unfamiliar surroundings, trying to assess her options in the dim light.

Across from the bus stop, she could see the faint, silvery sparkle of water. It looked magical and endless. She then spotted a sign for a Food Coop and a Country Market. Driven by hunger, she ran over to the market to grab something to eat and hopefully inquire about affordable places to stay for a night or two.

While she wandered through the aisles of the small store, she noticed several nuns quietly shopping. One of them, her kind eyes crinkling at the corners, approached her. "My child, do you happen to need some accommodations for the night?"

"Yes, Ma'am, I do, as a matter of fact," Aimee replied, a hopeful smile touching her lips. "I'm not sure for how long, but I promise I won't be any bother."

"We are just picking up some supplies for our convent," the nun explained. "You finish your shopping, and we can leave together, if this is agreeable to you. By the way, I'm Sister Ofelia, and these are Sister Hortencia and Sister Avila. We live at the new convent just up the road with seven other sisters, and we would be delighted to have a nice young lady like yourself as our guest."

"Thank you so much," Aimee said, a wave of relief washing over her. "I went to St. Agnes

Catholic School near Glassport when I was growing up."

"A very nice school," Sister Hortencia added with a warm smile.

They gathered their groceries and walked towards a van parked outside. As Sister Hortencia took the driver's seat, Sister Ofelia turned to Aimee. "We live at the Holy Family Monastery. We are the Carmelite Sisters, and we just arrived here last February. We do a lot of community work with the priests who live in the monastery and teach vocation and seminary classes. The ministry of prayer is very important to the life of our church here in northwest Pennsylvania. Every prayer is heard, even if someone is on an unexpected path or journey." She offered a gentle smile and kissed the rosary beads hanging around her neck.

Aimee returned her smile.

They arrived at the property, but it was difficult to distinguish its full appearance in the darkness. They each carried bags towards the dimly lit vestibule and then distributed the items to their respective places.

"While you are here, please feel free to ask us any questions you may have," Sister Avila said kindly. "To learn even more about our life here and around the world, we have several copies of our magazine, published by the Vatican's Congregation for Institutes of Consecrated Life and Societies of Apostolic Life. It might sound complicated and perhaps not too interesting to a young woman like yourself, but the articles are quite easy to read."

The nuns showed Aimee to a guest room. It was warm, cozy, and had immediate necessities. She expressed her gratitude to them all and closed the door. Just as Aimee was settling into bed, a gentle tap echoed from the door. She opened it to find a different nun holding a steaming cup of tea and a small plate of cookies. With a grateful smile, she accepted the thoughtful offering and quietly closed the door.

I Shot The Sheriff Meets Hurts So Bad

After a few months, it was time to get back to real life. Aimee thanked the nuns profusely for their unexpected kindness and the peaceful respite. She promised to visit again, and while the quiet rhythm of the nunnery was surprisingly comfortable – a place where she could have perhaps stayed indefinitely – the gentle yet persistent hints about becoming a nun had finally spurred her to move on. Three months had passed in their tranquil world, and she knew, deep down, she needed to find her own path again. Back to college, maybe.

She packed her accumulated clothes and goodies. As they lined up in ceremonious fashion, she offered each nun and priest heartfelt thanks and hugs for their generosity and unexpected joy of her adventure. They drove her to the local bus station where they first met. Sending her off with warm smiles and blessings, and she boarded the next bus heading south, a sense of both frenzy and anticipation swirling within.

She'd been meditating about her return to college and thought this would be a good time to see what credits she had, so headed back towards Washington and Jefferson to retrieve her transcript. She knew it wouldn't be much, but she had completed several classes before her short-lived university foray into her gypsy days.

After arriving, she walked across the familiar campus towards the records office, but a woman caught her eye. It was Marilu Grace. Both girls shrieked with surprise and went in for a tight hug.

"Aimee! Where have you been? I think about you so often." Marilu exclaimed, tears of joy sliding down her cheeks.

"Marilu. Oh my gosh! I've been up in Erie. I just needed a change, so I hopped on a bus. What are you doing here?" Aimee asked, her own eyes shining with happiness at the unexpected reunion.

"I'm here to apply for a job. It's finally time to quit cleaning houses," Marilu declared with a newfound sense of purpose. "You look so good. I always loved babysitting you back in the day. Hey, how long are you planning on being here? This is absolutely wild, but Glassport High School decided to throw a sort of reunion dance party for all the guys and gals who have been discharged from the service and have come back home. Please, please stay long enough to go with me. Please?" Marilu's enthusiasm was infectious.

"I didn't bring anything to wear. When is it? You are incredibly pushy, you know?" Aimee groaned playfully.

"It's this Saturday night at the old school gym, okay? You can borrow one of my dresses, or even better, we can go shopping for something totally wild. Yes? We can each get a brand-new mini skirt or dress. Maybe even some new shoes?" Marilu's excitement was bubbling over.

"It'll be kind of weird going without a date at nineteen," Aimee added.

"No, no, don't you even worry about it. It's a big group party. I won't have a date either. Besides, you're just as cute as you were back then, and there will be tons of people to dance with. We'll just have fun. I'm so excited, I might burst. The records office is just down the green hall. I should be finished here around four this afternoon, so I'll meet you in the cafe upstairs?" Marilu pointed towards the campus cafe overlooking the quad, then gave Aimee a quick wave, just like she used to as a spirited cheerleader.

Aimee felt like she had just been caught in a whirlwind, but she was genuinely happy about running into Marilu. She retrieved her academic records and headed to the cafe to grab a snack, looking forward to catching up with her old friend. Marilu should be done with her job application in about thirty minutes.

Saturday night arrived, and the girls were dressed in their new outfits, radiating youthful energy. Marilu looked vibrant in a green and yellow plaid mini dress paired with bright white Go-Go boots, while Aimee had chosen a bold floral print mini skirt with a sparkly, glittery top, adding height with four-inch leather heels.

As they pulled into the brightly lit school parking lot, an overwhelming number of people were showing up, making it clear this reunion party was definitely needed for this community. They were dressed in everything from casual to semi-formal attire. To pump up the excitement, the gymnasium was decorated with green and white cheer pompoms, streamers, balloons and a huge 7-0 adorned the stage. Because the dance included graduates from multiple years, most of the faces were unfamiliar to both girls. Aimee didn't recognize anyone unless Marilu specifically mentioned their names. They grabbed some punch, as sounds of laughter and excited chatter filled the air.

The mirrored glitter balls spun overhead, casting shimmering light across the dance floor as young and older alumni alike laughed and danced to the classic tunes like *"The Twist," "One is the Loneliest Number,"* and the whimsical notes of *"Puff, the Magic Dragon."* It was quite an eclectic mix of music. No one seemed lonely.

But then, Marilu suddenly jerked her body around, not in a dancing motion. Her face flushed crimson, and she grabbed Aimee's hand tightly. She was clearly on a mission, her eyes scanning the crowd with a focused intensity as she mumbled, "Why does a freaking forty-three-year-old man need to be at our school party?"

Aimee stopped her, her brow furrowed with concern. "What's going on, Marilu? You're all red. What is it?"

Marilu stopped abruptly, catching her breath and her eyes darting across the crowded gym. "Geez, oh my gosh, shit. I was almost positive I just saw that jerk, Karl Schmidt, the one who used to always hang around the cheerleaders. Your mom may have mentioned him and how he tormented little kids years ago." A shiver ran down her spine at the unwelcome flashback. "He was a big reason why your mom was so incredibly protective of you."

Aimee squeezed her arm and pulled her into a comforting hug. "Hey, we're here to have fun, remember? Let's try to forget about old creeps."

"Yes. Geez, that really scared me for a second. Let's get another drink." Marilu visibly tried to loosen up, accepting the cup of punch from Aimee. Luckily, she had a flask of magic in her purse that really calmed her down.

They enjoyed chatting with a few familiar faces, swaying their hips to the energetic beat of *"Kung Fu Fighting."* The lights then dimmed, signaling a slow dance, and the soft, sexy vibe of *"Crystal Blue Persuasion"* filled the gymnasium. It was a cozy and pleasant moment as couples crowded the dance floor, swaying gently in each other's arms. Both girls sighed.

But then, a faint, sharp scream cut through

the music. Both girls instinctively darted towards a nearby open door leading outside. There, in the dim light, they saw Karl Schmidt roughly shove Leona, a former cheerleader, to the ground. Marilu and Aimee both screamed for help. Several guys, hearing the commotion and not knowing what was happening, came running anyway. They grabbed Karl, who was yelling defensively about getting dirt in his eyes and threw him against a parked car outside. Ignoring his protests, the guys landed a few more punches before leaving him sprawled on the ground.

The girls rushed to Leona's side and helped her up, taking her back inside. She was physically okay but visibly shaken and distressed. Karl had ripped her new dress, so she desperately wanted to go home. Marilu quickly ran to get her car. They gently helped Leona into the front seat and drove away from the chaotic scene as quickly as possible.

To try and calm everyone down a bit, Marilu decided to stop for frosty twister cones at the local "Twister on Mon." Leona waited in the car while the other two went inside to get the ice cream treats. They all needed a sugary pick-me-up and some lighthearted laughter before taking Leona home. Marilu then drove to a quiet spot behind St. Cecilia's church, seeking a little extra peace on this unexpectedly crazy Saturday evening.

"You have to admit," Marilu said softly, licking her cone, "these ice cream cones used to make everything feel better when we were kids, so I say, why not now?"

The three girls enjoyed their treats in relative silence for a few moments. Then, Aimee started to giggle, a nervous release of tension. The other two soon joined in, their laughter echoing softly in the quiet evening air. Leona was feeling a little better, but still thought it best to head home. After getting her settled safely in her room without alerting her parents, the girls left. Marilu drove to a secluded spot near Glassport Hill Road.

"Okay, I have a plan," Marilu declared suddenly, her voice tight with sizzling anger. "It might sound hysterical, maybe even harsh, but it has to be done. If Heather and Heidi were here right now, I bet they'd agree with me. I am so sick and tired of how Karl has treated girls and women and even kids, ever since the awful creek incident with Scott Rand back in 1945, yet no one ever wanted to talk about it. You wouldn't remember it, Aimee, but he's always been a predator, and tonight just proved he hasn't changed and will never."

"Okay," Aimee said hesitantly, a knot of apprehension tightening in her stomach. "So, what's next?"

"Well," Marilu continued, her voice low and determined, "I still clean the Carmichaels' house, and they're all away in Waynesburg for a big football game. Mr. Carmichael has a gun, and I'm going to use it on Karl."

"What? Wait. What?" Aimee exclaimed, her eyes wide with shock. "Marilu, you can't do it. I'll do it. Let me do it." She squeezed Marilu's hand tightly. "I remember my mom hated Karl. He was always trying to get near me when I was little. Now I understand why she was always so overprotective. Tonight proved he'll never stop his sinister behavior, so I agree, he needs to be stopped. Let's do this together."

"Are you absolutely sure, Aimee?" Marilu asked, her gaze intense. "There's a special technique Grandpa Carmichael always used to talk about. If we're going to use his gun, I want to respect the fact we use it correctly, so Karl knows this is the absolute end. He's been a slithering snake in Glassport for way too long, and tonight was the final, disgusting straw. Let's go get the gun, and I'll tell you how to use it." Marilu took a deep breath and blew it out hard.

They drove to the Carmichaels' house. Knowing they were away, Marilu quickly ran inside, retrieved the old Beretta from its hiding place, and hurried back to the car.

"All these years," Marilu whispered, "I kept hearing about this being some kind of Mobster gun and the way they, well, the way they shoot people a certain way to make a point. It's too bad Karl's eyes might still have gravel in them because I'd almost enjoy knowing he saw the gun pointed right at him. Mr. Carmichael has told everyone 'this technique will send the right message.' We'll go over to his house, pretending we want to check on him. Hopefully, he'll be crumpled in a chair or collapsed on his couch. All you have to do is shoot him once, precisely in the heart, and then immediately right between his eyes. Got it? Here's the gun." She handed Aimee the heavy, cold metal. "It's kind of heavy. Make sure it feels okay in your hands."

"Sounds pretty simple," Aimee replied, her voice barely a whisper, the weight of the gun and the enormity of their plan settling upon her. "I just hope he's there."

They found Karl's dilapidated house. His beat-up truck was parked crookedly out front, and the dim light shone from the living room window. Marilu peered cautiously through the grimy window and saw Karl slumped in his armchair, an empty bottle of something dark resting on the floor beside him. She tried the front door; it was unlocked. She slowly pushed it open.

"Who's there? What the hell are you doing here? I can't see too good right now," Karl slurred, his voice thick with alcohol.

"Just the girls," Marilu said slowly, her voice deceptively sweet. "We wanted to check on you, Karl. Leona said she might have accidentally thrown some gravel in your eyes. It doesn't sting too bad, does it? Need a wet rag?"

"Get out. All of you. Get the hell out of my house!" he yelled, his voice rising in drunken fury.

Aimee raised the heavy gun, her hands surprisingly steady. She wasn't nervous or shaky, just a cold, hard resolve. This had to go as planned; he couldn't see clearly, and the overwhelming smell of alcohol confirmed he was in no condition to fight back. Marilu moved quickly behind his chair to straighten his head, then dashed silently back towards the open door, ready for their escape. As Aimee aimed the gun, her mind flashed back to all the times her mother had fearfully yelled at Karl to stay away from her. He was still a menace, still hurting people. She would end it.

Marilu turned her head with the escape route clear.

BANG!

BANG!

22~

Hunker Down Hideaway

Aimee was on the run again, the echo of the gunshots still faintly ringing in her ears, a strange lightness mingling with the gnawing anxiety clenched her stomach. The crime was thrilling, fulfilling in a way, giving some closure to anyone who needed it. But she knew the police wouldn't see it for the reason she did it. And now, her instincts pulled her back towards the quiet familiarity of Erie, her unexpected sanctuary.

She thoroughly enjoyed her time with the nuns, but this time she needed something different. Sin was greatly frowned upon by the church and she didn't want to bring any bad karma to the sweet, sweet nuns. Plus, maybe a place with less accessibility would be best.

Stepping off the bus in Erie, the familiar scent of woodsmoke and earth wafted across the street from the Amish community. She walked over to their simple community welcome tent and asked in a whisper, if they might have room for one more in their compound for a few weeks.

The leader, a man with a long, flowing beard and kind, yet discerning eyes, spoke with a deep, resonant voice. "Yes, daughter, you are welcome here. But you must understand, there are no forms of electronic communication allowed on our property. We are a self-sufficient people, finding our connection in the land and in each other."

Without hesitation, Aimee agreed. The absence of phones and computers, the complete disconnection from her past life, was exactly what she craved. This quiet, secluded world, where the rhythm of life was dictated by the seasons and the turning of the soil, felt like the perfect place to disappear, to begin the arduous process of starting over, knowing it might take a long time to truly find peace.

She introduced herself to the community as Mallory Jones. Her quiet demeanor and willingness to work hard, her hands quickly finding purpose in the simple tasks of their daily life, resonated with the leaders, who felt she would integrate easily. She was welcomed to stay indefinitely. She found a quiet joy in the predictable cadence of their days, the tangible connection to the land, getting her hands dirty seemed to soothe her restless spirit.

She was always happy to see the nuns at the market, and she grew to know the many new sisters who joined their ranks as the older ones gracefully retired from active community work, their eyes still holding a spark of joyful dedication.

As the years whirled by, marked by the changing seasons and the quiet growth of the community, Aimee, now Mallory, discovered new passions. Her favorite was the garden. The feel of the rich, dark earth between her bare fingers was deeply cathartic, a tangible connection to the cycle of life and growth.

One day as she knelt in the soft soil, preparing her raised beds for the planting, she overheard someone nearby remarking on how lovely the spring was.

Spring already, she mused, a gentle smile cracking her lips. Time had a way of slipping by unnoticed in this peaceful place, the days and years blurring into a comforting rhythm, yet sometimes leaving her feeling strangely adrift except while in the garden or with her son, Joseph. He would be graduating high school soon, a bittersweet milestone.

Joseph had inherited his father's inquisitive mind and his quiet yearning for the world beyond the familiar boundaries of their Amish community. He longed for the wider horizons of college, far away from the only home he had ever known.

"Depending on what you want to study, maybe we can see what's available around here, sweetie. Okay?" Aimee watched as Joseph sprinted off towards his classes. Twenty-five years, gone by. The realization struck her like a sudden jolt and a chilling awareness of the swift passage of time. Tears dribbled down her cheek like raindrops.

Goosebumps tickled her skin, a visceral reminder of the darkness she carried within, the ghosts still whispered in the quiet corners of her mind.

Joseph's youthful energy and quiet curiosity about the world beyond their community mirrored a desire Aimee herself had once felt, a yearning for knowledge and adventure beyond their familiar fields. Perhaps the most responsible thing she could do now, the truly grown-up decision, would be to honor his wishes, even if it meant confronting her own long-buried past. It was time to return to Glassport, to face her aging mother and the consequences of a life lived in the shadow of a single, irreversible act.

Raised within the strict traditions of the Amish community, Joseph's life had been defined by clear boundaries. Yet, Aimee could see the undeniable pull he felt from the outside world. She knew it was time for a serious conversation about her past. Joseph had inherited his father's inquisitive mind and longed for the wider horizons of college, far away from the only home he had ever known.

23

Carmichael Commentary

Back at the station the next day, Captain Grey placed a call to Walker Carmichael. "Mr. Carmichael, all your alibis have been thoroughly verified. However, since your father's gun has been identified as the murder weapon, we were hoping you might be able to shed some more light on the history of this firearm and who else might have had access to it. Yes, thank you." Grey hung up the phone, a thoughtful expression creasing his forehead.

"O'Malley," he said, turning to his lieutenant, "Walker Carmichael will be stopping by later for a chat."

Later in the afternoon, a visibly nervous Walker Carmichael arrived at the precinct, his knuckles white as he clutched his hands. Heather and Jack came with him for quiet support. Once they were seated in Captain Grey's office, Mr. Carmichael began to speak, his hands fidgeting in his lap.

"As I told you, Captain, my father brought his gun back from Italy after the war. He was in the Army during World War II. I know this might not seem directly relevant to your cold case, but I feel it's important for you to understand the kind of man my father was when he returned home. Most of the soldiers who came back were hardened, bitter, or just sad. But oddly enough, my dad was a genuinely happy man, and he became happily interested in food. My father was always kind and made friends easily. He discovered a small trattoria not far from the base where he was stationed. This family-owned eatery was always busy, but it was also a great place for him to learn about where the owners sourced their local ingredients. I think after having to eat Army C-rations for so long, he realized there was a much better way, even back then. The owners saw his genuine interest and took the time to teach him about the local farmlands and commercial fishing areas." Mr. Carmichael paused, taking a shaky breath, a sheen of tears in his eyes.

While Mr. Carmichael's recollections were indeed fascinating, O'Malley felt the need to steer the conversation back to the matter at hand. "Sir, this is all very interesting, but could we perhaps move along to the gun itself?"

Mr. Carmichael nodded, as he shifted in his seat.

"Yes, of course. So, some of the regular customers at the trattoria were rumored to be connected to the Mafia, but my father always described them as ordinary people, folks who walked their kids to school and went to church on Sundays. In turn, they could see my father was an honest and good man. They became quite attached to him and treated him almost like family. When the dinner rush at the eatery would slow down, the regulars would often gather and chat with each other. In one of the quieter conversations, some of the men described to my father how they dealt with troublemakers. Apparently, it was not uncommon to have to 'rough up' these idiots.

Those who openly admitted to being part of the Mafia said they only resorted to violence if someone threatened their families or their businesses. But some of these blockheads didn't learn their lesson the first time. As a result, and to send a clear message to the others, they would sometimes kill one of them to prove a point. Before my father was shipped out to come home, his new Italian family gifted him the gun, the one you have now, for his own family's safety here in America. But until yesterday, no one but us knew the gun's hiding place, tucked away and undisturbed, and we never had any reason to even look at it. Is this the kind of information you were hoping for, Captain?"

"Yes, sir, very insightful. We'll certainly take all of this under advisement, and I apologize if recounting those memories was exhausting for you," Captain Grey said, wiping his own brow, a deep sigh escaping his lips. "It sounds like both of your parents had a positive influence on your family's healthy eating habits, too, even if your children didn't realize the origins."

As the Carmichaels left the precinct, O'Malley turned to Captain Grey. "Hey, Cap, my wife's cousin at the library just called. She found some records indicating Glassport did indeed have some documented Mob activity here during the late 1960s and into the 1970s. Could it really be that simple?"

24

Sicily Substantiation

Walker Carmichael was a warm-hearted, family man who really wanted Captain Grey and Lieutenant O'Malley to know what kind of man his father was aside from the unfortunate gun issue. With genuine warmth, and knowing their time was valuable, Walker put his cherished memories in writing and sent them a copy:

My father's journey, so it began:

After my father returned from Sicily, he'd repeatedly say with an almost childlike enthusiasm, "fish and veggies, fish and veggies!" And our mother always agreed with a big smile because she knew he spoke the truth. He sounded like a walking encyclopedia because he had absorbed so much from the Italians. As we grew up, it seemed weird to us kids to have their father constantly recount his Army days in Sicily and want to tell everyone in Glassport, Pennsylvania about all the wonderful foods in Italy. But as I think back, we were very fortunate to have a dad who cared about what we ate. The encyclopedia man would report: 'Mt. Etna was a stratovolcano on the east coast of Sicily, Italy, in the Metropolitan City of Catania, between the cities of Messina and Catania.'

For him to take the time to learn the role of Mount Etna in Sicilian biodiversity was unheard of for a G.I. Most of his platoon didn't care what they were eating.

He discovered this volcano not only shaped the landscape but also created the ideal conditions for the development of a variety of endemic species and unique habitats. Thanks to its ongoing activity, Etna remains a natural laboratory where nature evolves and constantly adapts. Protecting this extraordinary heritage is crucial for the future of biodiversity in Sicily and for future generations who may care as much as he did. Mt. Etna wasn't just a volcano—it was described as the beating heart of Sicilian biodiversity.

He went back to the bustling, little bistro filled with the aroma of garlic and tomatoes every chance he got while he was stationed there, especially if he got to visit the pretty girl with a smile as warm as the Sicilian sun, my future mom, who worked there. He was a good man, and she was a great woman.

I really want to thank my parents for making me a lucky kid to have this kind of historical information. I was able to write several term papers and give presentations at school all because of my great father. The information was all about the positive effects of Mt. Etna's volcanic ash on fish production and farming and even learned volcanic ash waste products could be converted into resources, like bricks, for the construction industry. I had great parents. I think if he could have afforded it, we would've moved to Sicily, a special place clearly capturing his heart.

25 ~

Tides Have Turned

For what seemed like hours, O'Malley and Grey stared blindly at their rolling storyboard, the chaotic web of names and dates blurring before their eyes as the photos seemed to be staring back with unanswered questions.

But then, all at once, a jolt of realization seemed to physically lift them, and they both popped out of their chairs, the scraping of their chairs against the linoleum echoing in the silence.

"Wait a doggone minute. We have a murder weapon but still don't have a murderer." Captain Grey yelled, his voice echoing in the mostly empty office.

"You're right, Cap." O'Malley slapped his hand on his desk. "We have the weapon, its origin, the current owner, a self-described killer, but no shooter. Dagnabbit."

"I have an idea, Kelly. Gotta get all your persons-of-interest in here tomorrow in a group. We're gonna let them see each other face-to-face. Do it, O'Malley, 2 o'clock tomorrow right here."

Both men had their own possible suspect in mind, but lips were locked, their theories held close until tomorrow's meeting of the minds.

Lieutenant Detective Kelly O'Malley drove to every home of every person he'd interviewed. He always found more truth in those initial, unguarded reactions than in rehearsed answers, and he wanted to see the raw expression on their faces when they answered their doors and saw him standing there.

Upon arriving at each house, he used the same formal script for all:

"Kindly ensure your presence at the Glassport Police Department tomorrow promptly at 1:55 PM. We will convene upstairs near Captain Lance Grey's office. We have a few additional questions to ask but also respect the importance of your time and expect this meeting to be brief. Please be mindful of today's inclement weather. Boasting a sky the color of bruised plums and possible heavy rain and gusty winds predicted, take necessary precautions while traveling downtown. There will be plenty of parking. Your cooperation at such short notice is greatly appreciated."

26 ~

The Gang's All Here

As promised, the rain was mixed with snow making streets slushy and sidewalks mushy. One by one by 1:45pm, the motley crew started to arrive. As they headed up the stairway, they shook off umbrellas and raincoats and hung them on a rolling rack provided by one of the office clerks.

They all seemed to be a bit confused, panicky, and discombobulated to see others gathering in the same room. It was a hopeful idea, maybe some of them would recognize someone from their past or present.

There were plenty of chairs for the guests and plenty more for the extra officers asked to attend to take notes for Grey and O'Malley depending on which path this little roundup of Karl Schmidt's acquaintances or victims precipitated. It could be a beeline for the door, or a collision at the turnpike, or nothing. Like a poof of a dandelion.

But the inhouse officers, as well as street cops, had high hopes, and a few side bets, for any outburst. Their current beats were boring, they all needed some excitement, a little action.

Everyone was nervously present. A cup of water or coffee was offered. Then Captain Grey and Lt. O'Malley entered the room.

Lt. O'Malley stands in front. "Some of you know each other, but I'll do an intro for everyone's sake, especially for Captain Grey. He's seen your photos, but has only met a few of you. We're all frustrated we've spent so much time trying to find out who killed a sleazebag like Karl, but that's our job. Way too many guys like him give too many guys like us too many cases to solve, so let's just get this one done, if possible, today."

"Good afternoon, everyone. I'm Captain Lance Grey. Thank you for being prompt despite our universe's conscientious effort to mess up the roads and maybe your attitude. The reason you're all here is to give you one more chance to go over any last details that may have surfaced about the rat fink, Karl Schmidt. It's the truth. He was a bad guy in so many ways, and you all sadly encountered his outrageous, nauseating behavior in some form in your past or knew someone who did. This is an old, cold case and I really want it solved soon, but I need your help." Exclaimed Capt. Grey.

All heads were shaking yes or muffled yes words could be heard.

Earlier in the day, Kelly had positioned the chairs with name tags in a half circle for a more friendly feeling. He walked over and pointed to Scott Rand.

"Here in the center is Scott Rand. He was the little boy who Karl trampled with his horse at only 6 ½ years old. Scott survived, did join the Army, but his back pain from the horse trampling got so horrific and excruciating to serve his country, it forced Scott to request a medical discharge. He returned home and joined his father's lawn mower repair business down near the hardware and landscaping shop. Some of you may have used it. It is a small town. Please say hi to Scott."

A hush trailed a sad rumbling of voices, then the raising of a few eyebrows, succeeded by some waving.

"This is Heidi Drew Healy and her husband, Wayne. She was a high school cheerleader and was also a young acquaintance of Karl's but survived. Seems Glassport raised an amazing bunch of 'survivors of the fittest.' Heidi became a hairdresser after high school. Any of your aunts, moms, sisters frequent the shop near the old glass company property? It changed names a few times, but was Hairnet Harriet's for years, and then Tresses and Ten Pennies. Get it? Hair & Nails? Wayne was in the military and then retired from the fire department here. Please welcome them all to the group."

"Over next to Heidi, we have Marilu Grace. She didn't have much to contribute but knew and lived near Scott when they were young. They lived in the same neighborhood and attended the same school, but Scott was younger. She found out about Scott's accident after the fact. Marilu stayed in Glassport and joined her mom cleaning houses around town."

Walker Carmichael waved to Marilu. "I remember you used to help my wife clean the house. Thank you."

She smiled.

"Jody Larmi is next to Scott. She worked at The Cozy Cup coffee shop for years after high school to support her daughter. Anyway, she seems to be the only person in town who Karl actually bragged to about the incident with Scott. Karl thought if he acted like a big shot by telling her every gory detail, she might do something for him. His plan backfired, leaving him to scramble. Jody was a tough gal back then as a single mom. She reported having harsh words with Karl in regard to her daughter, Aimee. The local slimeball went after any young girl. She didn't have any reason to kill him, although knew where the gun was safely hidden at the Carmichaels."

Marilu got choked up a bit when she heard Aimee's name and the gun mentioned. It had been such a long time since they talked. O'Malley and Grey didn't notice, but one of the note takers did. The young officer needed to remember to report this to Captain Grey and Lt. O'Malley when this inquisition was finished. Could be a clue or nothing.

O'Malley continued with his introduction of guests.

"Jack, Heather and Walker Carmicheal are over on the end. Heather became an accountant at Washington and Jefferson where she and Jack went to college. Jack was a football linebacker, and she was a cheerleader. Jack joined the university staff as an engineer."

Captain Grey cuts in, "In a good way for us, but not so good for the Carmichaels, we did discover, after a lengthy investigative conversation and ballistics test, that Jack's dad's gun was, in fact, the murder weapon. Jack's grandpa brought the weapon back from Sicily when he left the military. It was a gift from some local friends who kind of adopted him. Jack's grandma came from there, too. Walker Carmichael worked at the city's sewer plant. Not a flattering position, but he made good money to pay for Jack's tuition."

"Thanks, Captain Grey, for this info. Ok, let's get back on track." O'Malley re-directs the goal of the meeting. "We all know Karl was shot to death but never revealed the actual manner he was killed. It's a grim revelation traditionally referred to as a Mafia Hit."

Gasps and heaves were exhaled. Shock filled the room.

"It's true and we wanted all of you to know now. An H&H, Head & Heart Hit involves the victim first being shot in the heart. Then the second bullet hits right between the eyes. This is so the victim lives just long enough to see the last shot coming. Just so you know, we had a strong circumstantial case against grandpa, Walker Carmichael's dad, but even if true, he's been dead for more than 30 years. So, we kept on digging. Come on, people. Got anything new?"

Captain Grey calls for a brief break, so the restrooms can be used, and ladies can freshen up. O'Malley heads into his office and Grey follows.

"Got any inklings, K.O.?"

"I think I feel a volcano beginning to erupt." Grey smiles at him and they return to the group.

"So, fine people of our quaint borough of Glassport, PA, do we have any takers or givers of information? You know this town has so many buried secrets, so let's lessen the burden of one today and we can all go home."

The room went silent. Sort of.

From the direction of the ladies' room, a very slight crying could be heard. From around the corner appears Heather 'Honey' Carmichael. Her eyes are bloodshot, and she tried to hold back her babbling. Jack runs over to her and embraces her. He brings her to her seat.

"Heather, is there something you remember or want to share?" Asks Lt. O'Malley.

"Yes, Sir. While Grandpa Carmichael was still alive, he showed me how to use his gun in case I was alone and needed protection. But then he died, everyone was sad, but I still remembered what he taught me. I was shopping in town one day and accidentally bumped into Karl at the market. He came up and grabbed my arm like he used to do at football games. Those memories flashed back to me. I pulled away from him, but he was raging mad. I went home and cried for quite a while. Then I devised a plan to meet him." She was sobbing heavily now.

Although probably not in police protocol, O'Malley went over and patted Heather's shoulder. Instead, she shoved his hand away and said,

"Let me finish. The next day, I got the gun from its safe place and went to Karl's barn trying to find him. He was there grooming his horse, so I did exactly what Grandpa Carmichael taught me to do. I did the deed and left the scene. When I got back home, I cleaned the gun and put it away and never thought about it again. It sealed a part of my life I was ashamed of, but this way he wouldn't bother any other kids or young ladies anymore."

By this time, everyone in the room was crying or clapping or both, including all officers, clerks, secretaries, and even the janitor who had secretly blended into the crowd to sneak a peek. This was a big deal. At last, an ancient secret was revealed, yet with it came the unsettling possibility. Was it resolved? Or not? The air was filled with confusion, mayhem, and chaos.

Mimicking a grade school musical chair bit, people began to scatter as the detectives directed employees to return to their respective workstations and all persons-of-interest were sent on their way. This conflicted moment demanded reflection, but the implications left them torn between satisfaction and apprehension. What just happened?

"Sirs?" said a sheepish voice from the stairwell area. "Can I come in for a minute?"

They both looked in that direction. It was one of the young officers brought in to take notes and survey the suspect gang.

"Sure, sure, what's your name, officer? O'Malley asked.

"Hi, I'm Duffield, one of your note takers." He looked nervous.

"Ok, then, Duffield, what can we do for you?" Conversed Grey politely.

"It's not what you can do for me, but what I did for you. Remember when you mentioned a girl, Aimee Larmi and the gun at the same time?"

Now both men sat straight up in their chairs. "What gives, Duffield?"

"The house cleaning lady you introduced, Marilu Grace, got a bit squirrely when you mentioned Aimee's name and then the gun. Not sure if it meant anything or if it was a knee-jerk reaction to hearing those two things in one sentence. I just thought you should know." Duffield picked up his notebook and got ready to exit.

"Great work, kid. Can we have your notebook page for our board? We greatly appreciate your attention to detail. You're on your way to being a great cop, maybe a detective? Thanks." O'Malley took the note and ushered him to the door.

A clue?

Or nothing more than a nervous reaction?

Exhaustion settled heavily in the room once more? Yes.

27 ~

Whodunit

The two detectives sat quietly at their desks for a bit. Silence enveloped them, yet their minds were anything but quiet, wrestling with the decision of where their efforts, maybe a conversation, just silence, would be most effective.

"So, what do you make of the latest epiphany? I think Heather's confession was sort of weak. I know we both have our own suspects in mind, so who'd you pin for the crime?" Captain Grey leaned back in his chair and put his shoes on the desk.

"You know, Cap, I figured it'd be one of the girls, Marilu or Jody, but not Heidi or Heather because they were out of town. Maybe Heather did it after they came home? They all had a weird history with Karl, all made questionable teenager and adult decisions, maybe some poor life choices, etc., but mostly because both Marilu and Heather had access to the gun at some point at the Carmichael home. Marilu cleaned the house, Heather married Jack, Jody was a single mom. Motive?"

"So where do we stand? Do we arrest her or let it rest for a day or so, O'Malley? What can the

D.A. do with this? Go home. Meet back here tomorrow morning." Grey plants his wingtip shoes on the floor, grabs his jacket, says good night and disappears down the stairs to the private officer parking lot.

It was Monday night and Captain Lance Grey loved to watch his team. He dashed home, threw his work clothes on the bed and donned a Steelers t-shirt. Tonight, it would be football. Tomorrow they would go in another direction, if needed.

Maybe a bit more legwork was needed. But where? Grey hadn't done actual legwork for years or been on beat patrol for decades. Although he loved the thrill of a chase, he had refined the much-needed finesse when dealing with suspects in person. He knew the importance of rubbing elbows with players of such groups such as today's clutch.

As a weathered figure in his sixties, he was only 5' 5", slightly hunched which spoke volumes of years he spent on the beat. His short salt-and-pepper hair highlighted piercing brown eyes framed by delicate crow's feet. His demeanor alluded to a lifetime of scrutinizing faces for cloistered truths.

Simultaneously with a Hail Mary touchdown, Grey was startled by the unmistakable sound of his well-worn leather jacket hitting the floor, but with an odd, clinking sound. As he bent over to retrieve the jacket, his eyes widened at the sight of his lucky charm lying on the floor beneath it. His dad's silver pocket watch flashed up at him in the light. It shouldn't be here, tucked in this jacket. Had he mistakenly left it in an inner pocket? When was the last time he even looked at it?

With an odd sense of tenacity prickling at him, he safely placed the watch in his dresser drawer, but what was this nagging tension in the air?

Over the watch?

Was it this cold case?

He shook his head knowing this investigation had worn out its welcome, but half-time was over.

Disoriented Divergence

Intermittent sunshine lightened and darkened the windows when Grey and O'Malley arrived at the office.

"I'm sure Heather has no worries about jail time, K.O., but she seems very unlikely for the killing due to her personality. Maybe she made it all up and is trying to protect someone else. We've been checking high school records up and down plus right and left, but maybe we should take a stab at nearby colleges, too. Maybe our searches have been too narrow especially on our timespan and locations."

O'Malley adds, "The Carmichaels reported they met while attending Washington and Jefferson which is approximately an hour southwest from here. Let's take a ride out there and see if anything pops up in their class rosters. It'll be nice to escape this office for a while. If we come up empty-handed, we'll look at Carlow University in Pittsburgh and then Pennsylvania Western up in the northeast. We didn't even think about trade schools and medical colleges. Back to college, Capt."

O'Malley & Grey gathered their notes and headed to the police parking lot where the cruiser was waiting. The lot mechanic filled it with gas and had it ready to go.

"K.O., you can drive."

They headed southwest to Washington, PA. With the school not far away, the drive was quick and peaceful. Looking at the school's site map, they located the admissions building and introduced themselves.

"Howdy, we're with the Glassport Police Department and we're investigating a cold case. Is there anyone who could assist us in looking up some old records? Maybe 1957-59-ish?"

"Welcome to Washington and Jefferson College, officers. Do you know who you are looking for or is this one of those needle-in-a-haystack situations?" The nice-looking gal smiled from behind the desk. "I'm Louise, but my assistant, Margie, will take you to our archive room. Most of our records are digital, but those years may still be on microfiche. There may be a few paper copies, too. Let us know if you need help. It can be daunting up there."

"Thanks." The men said in unison.

"Wow, this is amazing." Said O'Malley of the stacks and shelves and cabinets of records. His words bellowed through the archive room's tall ceilings. "Margie, can you point us in the direction of 1957-59 records?"

Margie pointed to a dark corner and excused herself.

"Cap, so what are we starting with? I can look up names like Jack and Heather, if you want to find cheerleaders. Does that work?"

"Sure." Agrees Grey.

O'Malley began his search with Heather Houston. She wasn't in the Class of 1952, so onto 1953. Here it is. A glossary of majors, students and Heather was listed. It wasn't a large class, so K.O. looked through all the names. "Hey, Cap, you doing ok over there?"

"Good to go, though nothing strikes me yet. Small group of college cheerleaders and I only recognize Heather. How about you? Anything?"

O'Malley popped up from the stacks of records and shared, "No gold nuggets here, so I'm just gonna scroll through and see if Aimee Larmi shows up anywhere. Maybe there's a sibling, aunt, uncle, someone who may be able to direct our search back home."

"Sounds productive." Says Grey.

"Holy Smokes. You're not going to believe who I found."

"Who, O'Malley, who?

"Aimee Larmi was listed as a freshman in 1969. She's a lot younger than the others but has now earned a spot on our suspect board. We haven't really asked anyone in our group if they've kept in touch or know her location. Not even her own mother claims to know of her whereabouts. It's like she just vanished. It may be coincidental, but her name has surfaced several times in the last few days now. Whatcha make of it?"

"I think it's time to do some digging in the Jody Larmi garden. Let's hope she opens up this time with a few better details. The other gals may have had a connection to her as well. What do you think, K.O.?"

"Let's do it." O'Malley agreed.

The guys furiously scribbled down every detail that may matter. Their pens were moving like lightning across the pages. With gratitude towards the records department gals for their invaluable assistance, they closed the door gently as they courteously bolted out the door. With adrenaline pumping through their veins and brains, they raced back to Glassport.

29

Monumental Modification

Aimee knew it was time for the truth to be told. It was going to be difficult telling Joseph, but it had to be done for the sake of their relationship and their future. She asked him to meet her out near their special tree after class. This is where his father, Atticus, was killed by a falling branch while loading his wagon. Magnificent in size, it remined them both of the strength and wisdom Atticus emulated. This wasn't for morbidity, but instead a safe place they both often went to talk to Atticus. She felt he needed to be included for the spiritual part and so he could sense the truth as well.

"Hey, Sweetie. How was class? Got homework?" She asked.

"It was an awesome lecture on accountability and how it determines success and failure in our lives. Mr. Nelson said accountability has to be consistently requested of everyone, all the time if you are to trust them. It made a lot of sense to me." Joseph said, as he looked up at the tree.

"It never ceases to amaze me what this universe can do and how it brings people together at exactly the right time." She smiled at Joseph. "I wanted you to meet me here so I could explain something from my past I'm not proud of, but it had to be done at the time. But instead of owning up to it, I ran as far away from Glassport as I could."

"Glassport? That's where you are from? I wish you would've told me this." Joseph started to sob for his mom and hugged her.

She nudged him away, so she could finish. "In 1970, I visited Washington and Jefferson College to get my transcripts and ran into Marilu, a gal who used to babysit me. It was great to see her again. She was there to apply for a job. She then told me the high school in Glassport was planning a celebration reunion dance for G.I. gals and guys who were returning home, and I should come."

"Ok, mom, what?" Asked Joseph. "I don't understand."

Aimee continued, "Ok, hold on a minute for me to explain. I did go with her. All the girls were dressed up and having a great time, but Marilu thought she saw this jerk who used to harass little kids and flirt with cheerleaders. We went back to the dance floor and the lights went dim for a slow dance. We didn't notice right away, but he sneaked into the school gym. He grabbed one of the girls tight and dragged her outside. Supposedly, they had a past. We all heard a scream outside an open door and found Leona struggling to get away, but this guy Karl had a tight grip around her body. He pushed her down to the rocky, gravel parking lot and started to rip her clothes. Grabbing a handful, she threw it in his face. She screamed and a group of boys ran outside to help. We grabbed Leona and the guys beat Karl up a bit. We then told the school police and took Leona home. We both felt we had to do something. Marilu was more upset and said her blood was boiling."

Joseph just sat in the grass dumbfounded. He didn't know how to react or respond because only knew his mom to be kind and gentle. But he also knew they would get through this and be better for it...hopefully.

30

Chaos Continues

The next morning, the rented car was packed up and they were ready to go. Aimee thanked the community for being her safe haven. She explained she wasn't sure they'd be back anytime soon.

It was time for Aimee to face the music.

Aimee was driving and Joseph was reading the map. It was an easy trip down Hwy 79 south. The same highway that transported her twice to her new life, 25 years ago. It would take them right to Glassport. And oddly, they would be there in just over two hours. So close, yet so far.

There wasn't much talking until Aimee shared how she traveled to Erie back then before the dance incident. She told Joseph about the kind people she met along the way including the lady at the store who gave her warm cookies for her journey, and Clarence. She told Joseph how sweet he was to let her stay for a few days, had given her a better map for the trip, and a few bucks for the road.

If not for being so discombobulated and distraught, she might've trusted her mom to help with this serious debacle. But being youthful, she explained, sometimes dumbs the brain causing all reality and accountability to dissipate into thin air.

Later that morning, Captain Grey and K.O. met back at their offices, "Just some official paperwork and we're done. When a case is this old, we take what we can get and move on, O'Malley. No charges will be filed on Scott or Heather for false confessions."

Almost immediately, there was a knock on the closed door.

"K.O., Captain Grey, there's a lady downstairs in the lobby looking for a detective. Should I send her up?" said the front desk sergeant.

"Did you get a name or ask what she needs?" asked Grey.

"Sir, she said her name is Aimee Larmi."

Astonished, both men leaped out of their chairs, almost running over the sergeant as they dashed downstairs. The officer safely flattened himself against the wall to let them pass without anyone getting hurt.

When they reached the lobby, a mesmerizing woman was sitting next to a young man. She could be an identical twin to her mom, Jody Larmi. Approaching cautiously and politely, they both greeted her.

"Hello, I'm Aimee Larmi and I need to talk. This is my son, Joseph."

"Well, wonderful. I'm Captain Grey and this is Lt. Kelly O'Malley. Pointing at the stairs, Grey led, and O'Malley followed with the teenager. K.O. proceeded to the vending machines as a distraction for the kid, and Captain Grey invited Aimee into his office, closing the door.

"Want a snack, young man?" O'Malley pointing at the machines. Joseph affirmed the offer.

"It's nice to meet you, Aimee. Your name just came up on our investigative radar, but we had no idea where you could be. Your mom had no clues, high school friends never mentioned you. What happened at college to make you disappear, um, 25 years ago?"

"Well, Captain Grey, I killed Karl Schmidt in 1970."

Silence hung heavy as the captain's eyes got big. K.O. entered the room and said, "What did I miss?"

"Aimee, would you like to repeat your last statement?"

"Yes, sir, I killed Karl Schmidt in 1970."

Now K.O.'s eyes were as huge as half-dollars as he exclaimed, "Wowzers! We've been working this cold case for weeks. You may be the answer we've been looking for."

"Yes, sir, I'm sorry to have caused you frustration, but I figured with my son looking at colleges, it'd be best to clear the air, and tell the truth no matter what happens to me."

The men looked at each other for what to say next. Silence again.

"Aimee, have you been using that name you've been using all these years?" asked Grey.

"No, sir, I lived with the nuns in Erie for a few months and then ended up in an Amish community but told them my name was Mallory Jones. Not really creative, but it worked then. In the monastery, silence is golden, and at the compound, documentation was seldom used and there was no electronic communication allowed. I felt safe, invisible. But with Joseph growing up and wanting to visit colleges, I thought it best to come clean. I do not regret what I did. Karl was so brutal, simply scary to be around. When he attacked Leona at the dance reunion, Marilu and I couldn't contain our emotions."

"Wait. What? Who? Attacked someone named Leona? And Marilu? She never divulged that detail nor did a gal named Leona come up. We need to make some calls." O'Malley's outburst could be heard throughout the second-floor offices. Some employees rushed from their offices to see what was happening.

"Hold on, Lt., let's get the entire story before we start calling people in." Captain Grey tried to be the calm one. "Aimee, here's your chance to explain yourself. Take all the time you need."

Aimee asked for some water and wanted to check on Joseph. O'Malley assured her of his safety. She began the dissertation.

"Aimee, we are disgustingly aware of Karl's

despicable behavior and how he bullied many kids, but did you consider turning yourself in back then? You realize this was serious. I do applaud your decision to come in now, but I can't guarantee the outcome." Captain Grey scratched his chin and pondered their next step. "Let's first call your mom. I think she deserves to be the first person to see you and to meet her teenage grandson. Deal?"

"Yes, Captain, but I was 19 and Erie was a safe haven where no one asked questions about anything. And it was the end of the bus route. Dilemmas are solved if you trust the universe." Aimee agreed to the idea of contacting her mom. She and Joseph waited in Captain Grey's office.

"K.O., can you go out to Jody Larmi's house and ask her to come back in? I want you to give her a 'no lights, no sirens' police escort to the precinct, but assure her there's no issues with her statement. We just want to show her something."

While Aimee and Joseph anticipated Jody's arrival, they both dozed off on the comfy, leather sofa in Grey's office.

O'Malley headed to Jody's place with another squad car following. He knocked.

"Hi, Lt. O'Malley. Is everything ok? Why is there another police car here? Am I in trouble?" She said frantically.

"No, no, Jody. We just have something at the office we'd like to show you. Can you drive over with us? I'll lead and Officer Borowitz will follow. This way we all get there at the same time."

"Ok, but this is shaking me up." She gathered her purse and keys.

"It's gonna be ok, I promise, you." Smiled O'Malley.

They cruised down Glassport Hill, passed the fire station, post office, along the river and passed the old glass company property. They all parked in the officer parking lot and entered through the back door. O'Malley bounded up two stairs at a time and waited for Jody at the top where he held the door.

"This is all very scary for me." She was trembling as her voice cracked a little.

When Jody arrived, she saw the bulletin board the men had been using for the cold case investigation. It showed pictures and names of all the people who were gathered there. But then she saw Aimee's name. "Why is my daughter's name on your board?"

Gently, Grey held her arm and said, "Jody, we're sorry to have rattled you, but her name just popped up while we were investigating some files at Washington and Jefferson College. We just discovered it yesterday, but something happened today we'd like to share with you. How about chat? Would you like to sit?" She shook her head yes for both questions.

Then Captain Grey went to his office door and slowly opened it. He motioned to Aimee to come out.

Jody had been looking down in fright but looked up and screamed. "Aimee, Aimee, Aimee, where have you been? Oh my God, I've missed you so much. I can't believe this. Captain Grey, thank you, thank you."

She and Aimee hugged and cried, then cried some more and hugged, and sniffled for what seemed like an hour. Then out of the room, Joseph appeared. Jody stared. Aimee let go of her hand and reached for Joseph's. "Mom, this is your grandson, Joseph."

Again, with the tears and the sobbing outbursts, and hugs and then three people just staring at each other in a soggy silence. Captain Grey motioned for everyone to come into his office. This would be more private.

"So, Jody, Aimee just showed up this afternoon with a tale to tell. Something she had to come clean about. Does anyone need a refreshment, a snack? This may take a while. We'll let you chat here in my office while we contact Marilu and Heather. Sound reasonable?" asked Grey.

"Marilu? Heather? Why them? What's going on?" Blubbering, Jody questioned.

Lt. O'Malley assured her it was just a formality. If they needed anything, they'd be in O'Malley's office. Grey and O'Malley left the room and went to a quiet corner. "We know both of those women need to come back in for a redo interrogation. You want to go round them up and bring them back here?" asked the captain.

"You want both at once?" speculated O'Malley.

"We need to drill Heather into why she gave us a false confession. It was probably meant to protect Wayne. But Marilu owes us an explanation for keeping the attack a secret. Let's bring one gal in at a time." Grey sat down as Kelly left.

This case just became very chaotic, but they were both finally seeing an end to it. Just have to get the players to stay in their lanes and tell the truth.

Grey could hear Aimee explain, so peeked in the door.

"He was such a bully to so many kids. Marilu and I decided in the heat of the moment at that dance, we wouldn't let him torture anyone again."

Joseph grinned ear to ear even as tears streamed down the women's faces. Their eyes sparkled with joy. The emotional weight of the moment was tangible but eerily spirit-lifting as they all sat in wonder of what their futures held. The family was reunited at last, a circle once broken, now whole again, and they could envision the promise of a fresh beginning.

Cold Case Chaos Cancelled

The next morning, both men looked refreshed when they arrived at the office.

"I'll send my report to the mayor and the chief and wait for a reply, but, Kelly, it's time to send this COLD case to the deep FREEZE. There's not much else to say unless they want to charge Aimee Larmi with the murder, but I'm positive it won't happen. She rid our town of a virus."

"The mayor thanked us for the good work. As promised, here's that big, fat bonus. Scott Rand will also get a reward. Without his help leading back to Heather *'Honey'* Carmichael, we would still be chasing our tails. Any firm plans for retirement yet, K.O.? Or maybe you like to take a shot at Chief Mooney's new list of cold cases? He thought since you've revitalized, or better yet, perfected your cold case skills, you'd be ready to take on another one."

"Well, Cap, let me overthink the offer. NO way. I'm out of here as soon as I can get my paperwork filed, my desk cleaned out, and my bags packed for sunny Florida. Most northern retirees I've known fly south, buy a condo and a Buick."

"That's very funny, K.O. You better watch out for those spring break beauties. You know what chasing young bikinis can lead to."

"Captain, my wife will be my captain now. It will be a treat to relax with her. No bikinis or cheerleaders for me."

"K.O., I won't be far behind you. I'll get the condo next to you, but I'll keep my Ford. We can reminisce about the good old days before Cold Case Chaos."

As K.O. left the Glassport Police Department for the last time, he thought a stroll by the river would be a great way to wind down before arriving at home. He often daydreamed what the town was like back in the glass company days. He couldn't even fathom the human strength and expense it took to work the furnaces or the old water tank. Those employees earned their keep until their jobs abruptly ended. Lucky for Glassport, those easy-to-find tiny, shiny shards will forever be embedded in its history, its landscape, its rivers.

As he got to a shallow place in the water, the evening sun reflected something on the river's edge. He put his briefcase down and decided to jockey himself over the rickety fence to see what it was.

Holy shit, holy shit! He repeated over and over. He was exhausted, so was very untrusting of his eyes. He moved some of the river's edge dirt and grabbed the glistening rock and stared. Not a rock, but a perfect piece of green glass in the shape of a 4-leaf clover.

How the heck could this happen? I'm torn

between calling it the luck of the Irish or just pure coincidence. Luck of the Irish is my guess. He snickered.

Tucking his treasure securely into his pocket, he carefully maneuvered back over the fence. His movements were uncoordinated and not something an old man should be doing. Once safely on the other side, he adjusted his jacket and picked up his briefcase.

The sun was setting on this retirement day, so he adjusted his Bilby against the glare. The evening air cooled gently against his skin as he set off on the familiar path toward home.

The End

BIOS:

Conrad Case attended McKeesport High School near Glassport, PA; he then enlisted in Navy Reserves in 1957. After his service, he worked various types of employment such as truck driver, cab driver; and worked on an Ore Carrier on The Great Lakes, Superior and Michigan. Case has worked and resided in the Reno, NV area for decades. In 2024, he enlisted Peggy Rew's help in ghostwriting this Pennsylvanian mystery, but they promptly became co-writers.

M. Peggy A. Rew is *All Things Pets with a Wordsmith Twist* based in Sparks, NV. Always in graphospasm, Rew has authored 100s of articles, taught wordsmith classes and wrote two *Dog Bite Prevention* books, plus poetry and shorts for *Sections of My Grapefruit*. She's been a freelance journalist and ghostwriter; and professional pet nanny and pet care educator for 40+ years.